REDONDO BEACH P

S0-AFN-190

Aaron
minn

BK
BGO

Dragon's Milk

Dragon's Milk

Susan Fletcher

Aladdin Paperbacks

If you purchased this book without a cover you should be aware that this book is stolen property. It was reported as "unsold and destroyed" to the publisher and neither the author nor the publisher has received any payment for this "stripped book."

First Aladdin Paperbacks edition 1992
Copyright © 1989 by Susan Fletcher
Aladdin Paperbacks
An imprint of Simon & Schuster
Children's Publishing Division
1230 Avenue of the Americas
New York, NY 10020
All rights reserved, including the right of
reproduction in whole or in part in any form.
Also available in a Atheneum Books for Young Readers edition.
Printed and bound in the United States of America

25 24 23 22 21 20 19

Library of Congress Cataloging-in-Publication Data
Fletcher, Susan, 1951–
Dragon's milk / Susan Fletcher. — 1st Aladdin Books ed.
p.   cm.
Summary: Kaeldra, an outsider adopted by an Elythian family as a baby, possesses the power to understand dragons and uses this power to try to save her younger sister, who needs dragon's milk to recover from an illness.
ISBN 0-689-71623-0
[1. Dragons—Fiction.   2. Fantasy.]   I. Title.
PZ7.F6356Dr   1992
[Fic]—dc20   91-31358

For Jerry and Kelly

acknowledgments

I gratefully acknowledge Frank Irby at the Pacific Northwest College of Art, as well as Yothin Amnuayphol and Cheryl Guggenheim, for showing me the potter's art. I am also indebted to Peter Dickinson's *The Flight of Dragons* for the anatomy of dragon flight.

Thanks to Becky Huntting for her excellent proofreading of the manuscript.

Thanks, too, to all the members of my two critique groups for valuable criticism and moral support; and particularly to Eloise McGraw, who took time to read and comment on the entire manuscript.

I'm especially grateful to my husband, Jerry, and my daughter, Kelly, for inspiration and for their unflagging patience and faith in the project.

Finally, heartfelt thanks to Ellen Howard for her generous help at every stage of this book, and for the word "draclings."

Dragon's Milk

chapter 1

And when the draclings hatch, the sire-drake roars
so as to tremble the earth. He spirals into the sky;
he looses the wind and the thunder and the hail.
Nor keeps the dam-drake silence, but, abandoned,
wails most piteously; and thus abates the storm.
—*The Bok of Dragon*

Something was wrong.

Kaeldra knew it the moment she awoke. She sat bolt upright and strained her senses against the dark. The loft smelled of mildew and damp hay. A cold breath of mist wrapped around her shoulders and neck. Something—the seabird?—rustled in the room down below. Beside her, Kaeldra heard Lyf's soft snoring. She reached out and laid her hand on Lyf's chest and felt reassured, somehow, by its gentle rise and fall.

Gradually the blackness in the loft dissolved into vague gray shapes. Now Kaeldra could make out Mirym's sleeping form in the far corner, could see the dark half-

1

circles of Lyf's lashes against her cheeks.

Everything all right. No sign of what had awakened her. No hint of anything wrong, except the prickling chill that crept up Kaeldra's spine and fanned out across her back.

From far away came the bleat of a sheep, deep and mournful. Then two more, almost together, right after. They were restless, as she was, tonight.

The sheep. It was not yet lambing time, although sometimes there was an early snow-lamb. The Calyffs had had one last year. But Kaeldra had been watching, and none of the ewes was ripe for lambing.

It was nothing. They were restless, that was all.

Another bleat. Then another, and another. An overlapping of bleat upon bleat, coming slowly at first and then faster and fuller.

It was something!

Kaeldra threw off her blanket and pulled on her cloak. She thrust one foot into a fur-lined boot and had just begun to tie its leather thongs when she heard the door open below.

There were footsteps inside, then a voice, dry and urgent and low. Granmyr. A stirring of straw, then Ryfenn, Kaeldra's second-mother, spoke, whining and afraid. "Must we *now*? Why could we not—?" Kaeldra heard; then Granmyr's voice, short and sharp, cut her off. Kaeldra crept to the edge of the loft and leaned over. The two women's shapes hunched over something on the floor, and then the cock crowed and the seabird shrieked, beat its wings against its cage. And the chickens

2

were squawking and the goose was braying and the sheep were bleating all at once. Two soft arms slipped around Kaeldra's waist, and she looked down into the small white oval of Lyf's face.

"Kael, what is it?"

"I don't know, Lyfling," Kaeldra said. She crawled away from the edge of the loft and hugged Lyf to her. Mirym knelt, uncertain, in the corner. "Kael—?" she began, and then she ran across and laid her head on Kaeldra's shoulder, something she had not done in twelvemoon, not since she had turned eleven and had got so smart.

Kaeldra wrapped her arms around Lyf and Mirym. They were trembling, Lyf and Mirym, and then Kaeldra, too, because they were trembling against her. No, it wasn't Lyf and Mirym at all, but something else: the loft trembling against her legs, the air trembling against her back and face, the whole world trembling, vibrating, humming. She heard it with her body, not with her ears, and then it was in her ears, too, a rumble like distant thunder that grew louder and louder until it sang in her teeth and bones.

"Kaeldra! Bring them here!"

Granmyr stood on the ladder at the edge of the loft. Kaeldra crawled to her, Lyf and Mirym clinging. She lifted Lyf and handed her to Granmyr; they disappeared down the ladder. Then Mirym climbed onto the ladder. It shook and chattered against the edge of the loft; Kaeldra held on to steady it as Mirym went down.

Kaeldra was on the ladder now. It shuddered and

creaked. Gray orbs were streaking through the dark. They made soft popping noises when they hit the floor. Pots. Granmyr's ceramic pots, falling from the shelf. Then came a *crack!* and Kaeldra was falling. The floor lunged up and smacked against her shoulder and now the humming was so loud it was a roar, flooding the house, drowning out the sheep and the chickens and the goose. Kaeldra clapped her hands over her ears, but the roar kept on rising, almost human, exultant.

And then it stopped.

"Get down here! Now!" Granmyr's voice sounded loud against the dwindling chorus of bleats and clucks. She stood near the open cellar door waving her arms.

"Kaeldra! Now!"

Kaeldra blinked. Why was she doing that? It was all over now, the trembling, the hum, the roar. Why was she yelling? Why was she waving her arms?

The wind came up out of the east, from the mountains. It screamed down the rocky slopes, tore across the graze, slammed into the house, and ripped off a chunk of roof. Thunder boomed; Kaeldra jumped up and ran for the cellar. Hailstones bounced and slipped under her feet. She followed Granmyr through the hole in the floor and down another ladder. The cellar door thudded above her. Kaeldra stood there a moment, hugging herself in the dark. Her shoulder ached where it had hit the floor. Her bootless foot tingled with cold. Then something warm and soft pressed against her—Lyf—and Kaeldra folded herself around the child.

"You're dressed." Granmyr's voice came, close to her ear.

"I—I felt something."

"Ah," Granmyr said. She touched Kaeldra's arm. "Listen."

Outside, the wind howled. The cellar door shook with the rattle of hail. Somewhere to her left, Kaeldra heard Ryfenn, moaning. Kaeldra's own heartbeat sounded loud in her ears.

And then—there it was.

High-pitched and plaintive, a new sound twined around the wind wail. It mingled at first, then, growing, dominated, hushed the wind entirely. It was not a human sound, but the feelings it voiced were human. There was triumph in it, but also the underside of triumph: regret, loneliness, despair.

It rose, a great soul-sung lament, then all at once it, too, fell silent, its echo retreating back across the moors into the mountains. And in the hush that followed, Kaeldra heard, or thought she heard, the pulse of a giant wingbeat, flying east.

chapter 2

To play host to the *farin* is to warm the wolf at your hearth.

—Elythian proverb

The gods are punishing us."

Ryfenn's voice was stretched taut. She swept the floor with quick, hard strokes.

Through the hearth smoke Kaeldra watched, warming her hands at the fire.

"The gods had nothing to do with it," Granmyr said. She dug a lump of clay from her bowl, wedged it, slapped it onto her claywheel. Her right foot, shod in its heavy boot, kicked the spinner. Whirling, the clay sprang up, a smooth, grooved dome beneath her hands.

"Don't say such things," Ryfenn hissed. "We will pay. We are paying now."

6

Paying for what? Kaeldra wondered. Heat seeped into her cold-numbed body: her toes, the fronts of her legs, her face.

Granmyr touched two fingers to the center of the dome, saying nothing. The dome hollowed out and was suddenly a bowl, with tall, sloping sides growing up out of it.

Daylight had huddled near the mountaintops when Kaeldra went out to care for the sheep after the storm. She had followed the shape of the land to their shelter places, near the rocks. But the sheep had not sought shelter. They were scattered across the graze. When they saw Kaeldra, they bleated stupidly and did not move.

All morning, as the mist bleached the sky to the color of washed wool, she had roamed the graze. There were strange, glazed whorls and ridges in the snow, as if it had melted, churned, then frozen again.

And seven sheep were dead. More than they had ever lost to wolves in a single night.

Kaeldra turned to warm her back at the fire, trying to shut out the images of the dead sheep: four trampled, two crushed by falling rocks, one dead of fright. Her body ached from the effort of gathering together the live ones, of hauling the dead ones on a sled to be skinned and butchered at home.

"It's more than I can bear," Ryfenn said. "All alone here, with no one to help me, and no Bryam . . ." Ryfenn's voice got whiny and her eyes watered up as they always did when she mentioned her dead husband, Granmyr's son.

"You have Kaeldra," Granmyr said.

Ryfenn flicked her eyes toward Kaeldra, then away.

"Ryfenn," Kaeldra said. "I'll help. What should I do?"

Ryfenn did not look at her. Her broom swished hard against the floor. Kaeldra, watching, felt a small, hollow place open up below her ribs.

"Go to the loft and look to Lyf. She's not feeling well," Granmyr said.

Kaeldra hesitated. There was a question she had been turning over in her mind. She had waited, thinking someone else would ask it, but no one had. "Granmyr," she began at last, "what were the cries? The cries I heard last night in the storm?"

Ryfenn looked up sharply. "What cries? There were no cries." She turned to Granmyr. "She heard cries! I told you, she's—"

"To the loft, child," Granmyr said. She kicked the spinner. The clay bowl whirled.

Stung, Kaeldra climbed the ladder, up past the broken rung to the loft. It's not fair, she thought. Not fair of Ryfenn not to like me. She never likes me, even when I help. And I *do* help. I help a lot.

Lyf lay curled in the straw, her face soft and slack in sleep. Lyf was not feeling well, Granmyr had said. Kaeldra sat down, brushed back Lyf's hair from her forehead. It felt warm, too warm, and damp.

She wouldn't ask that Ryfenn love her, not the way she loved Lyf and Mirym—they were her birth-daughters, after all. They were easy to love. But if only Ryfenn would like her, or at least appreciate the things she did. If once she would say thank you.

Below, the steady hum of Granmyr's claywheel stopped. It was strange to hear it here in the cottage. But the storm had pulled down Granmyr's clayhouse, and there was nowhere else to put it. Kaeldra heard a scraping sound, then the thud of the pot being set on a plank to dry.

". . . ever since you took her in, when that mother of hers died," Kaeldra heard Ryfenn say.

"Shh," Granmyr said.

Her boot thunked against the spinner, and Ryfenn's voice, low and insistent, continued, masked by the noise of the wheel. Kaeldra rolled onto her stomach, cleared the straw from the boards and pressed her ear against a crack.

"You cannot deny she is strange," Ryfenn was saying. "Just look at her. So tall, already taller than any of our women and most of our men. And her hair. No Elythian has hair that color. No Elythian's hair crinkles like hers. And her eyes—they are *green*."

"So?"

"She is *farin*! Of the Krags! She doesn't belong here—we are paying the price. Just look at all that has happened since she came. The drought and the stillbirths and my poor Bryam—"

"Don't be ridiculous," Granmyr said. "Kaeldra had nothing to do with Bryam's death, or anything else."

". . . and now that storm. Seven sheep! There's something evil up there in the mountains, and Kaeldra *knew.* She was already dressed. And the cries she spoke of, what of that?" Ryfenn's voice cracked, came out high and harsh. "She's *communing* with it."

"Shush, Ryfenn! Stop it."

Granmyr's boot thunked hard against the spinner. Kaeldra lay paralyzed. Something was breaking apart inside her. Ryfenn thought that she—that Kaeldra—had made the bad things happen.

Granmyr's voice came again, so low Kaeldra could barely hear. "Kaeldra was not the only one. I sensed it, too, but could not place it; could not hear the cries."

"Sensed what?" Ryfenn hissed. "Mother, what *is* it?"

The wheel sounds diminished, as if Granmyr had forgotten to kick the spinner. When she spoke, her voice was soft and distant, as if she had forgotten Ryfenn, too, and spoke only to herself. "Nearly sixty years it's been, and now—"

"What? What *is* it?"

The door banged open. The house hens fluttered and clucked.

"A wizard!" It was Mirym. "There's a wizard in the mountains!"

Kaeldra scrambled down the ladder. Mirym's cheeks were flushed pink; her breath came in short gasps.

"Wynn says he's from Kragrom," Mirym said. "Their armies couldn't push through the mountains so they sent their most powerful wizard instead, the Lord High Magician of all of Kragrom."

Granmyr snorted. She kicked at the spinner, and the wheel began to move.

"I knew it," Ryfenn moaned. "What will he do to us?"

"Wynn says he's going to visit us with storms for seven nights and seven days," Mirym said cheerfully. "That's what he did to the Ulians. He destroyed all their crops and livestock, and they had to surrender."

Ryfenn moaned again.

"Don't worry, Mother. The men are mustering a war party for the glory of Elythia."

"A war party!" Ryfenn wailed. "That's how my Bryam died!" Ryfenn began to weep.

"Glory," Granmyr muttered. "Always running off to get themselves killed."

"They're leaving at first light tomorrow. Wynn is wearing my amulet!"

"Your *what*?" Ryfenn stopped crying. "You're too young to grant your amulet!"

"Mother! Wynn is going to *war*! I may never see him again. Anyway, all the other girls are doing it. Ellyr granted hers to Styfan, and Rymig granted hers to Yoland. Everyone over twelve years old has granted her amulet toda—" Mirym looked guiltily at Kaeldra, then at the floor.

Kaeldra felt the warmth rising in her face. Mirym had granted her amulet! And so had all the other girls, everyone over twelve, Mirym said, except—Kaeldra swallowed hard.

Farin. Ryfenn had called her *farin*, and it was true. Even her name sounded Kragish. She was not of the Elythians; she was different; she did not belong.

For as long as she could remember, she had tried to

11

be like the others. She had watched how they did things, always following, always moving a half beat behind so as to get it right: the turn of hand, the tilt of head, the lift of voice. She wove her gown in the Elythian way, dyed it in the pale pastels they wore, and cut it long, so as not to look so tall.

Kaeldra wore her hair in the Elythian way, too, in a plait down her back, past her waist. It was thick and soft, but much too light; it twisted and coiled like a hank of sheep fleece. She combed it and smoothed it, but the coils would not unbend. Why couldn't her hair be like the Elythian girls' hair, sleek and black as a raven's wing?

Except in dreams, when unfamiliar voices drifted in and out of her ken, Kaeldra could not remember what it was like to be anything but Elythian. She had been told that she came here from Kragrom with her mother when she was five. Her mother had died; Granmyr took her in. And through the years Kaeldra had convinced herself that the things she could not change—her height, her hair, her eyes—did not matter.

She had been wrong, of course. They did matter. Because of pairing, they mattered.

It was a year ago, when Mirym was eleven, that Kaeldra had known. Mirym was pouring brew at the fair, and Wynn had looked at her in a new way. No one had ever looked at Kaeldra that way. And she had been fifteen.

Boys liked Mirym. They liked little, lithe girls, with lilting laughs like Mirym's. And, much as Kaeldra told herself she was just an early grower, it was clear that she could never be little or lithe. She towered over the boys;

they avoided her. She felt awkward, overgrown.

And now Ryfenn was thinking—communing with it, she had said. And Kaeldra *had* felt something last night, even before the sheep. She *had* heard the cries. What if she *were* communing with an evil thing, a wizard? What if there were something inside her she couldn't control, like when she kept growing and growing and couldn't stop—

"Kaeldra!" Granmyr said.

Startled, Kaeldra turned.

"Get the red clay."

Kaeldra lugged the stout clay-crock to Granmyr, who pulled a cutting thread beneath the base of the gray bowl she'd just finished and set it on a plank to dry. Seldom did she work the red clay, although she favored it, for the trip to get it took three days.

Granmyr reached into the crock and began wedging a hunk of clay. "Time it is," she said softly, "to see if I am right." Looking up at Ryfenn and Mirym, she added, "You need tell no one of this. Though I doubt that they would credit it. Not yet."

The old woman sat still for a long moment, her hands resting in her lap. Then she nudged the spinner with her unbooted foot, and the wheel began to circle— not in its usual direction, but the other way. Slowly it moved, and then faster, faster than Kaeldra had ever seen it go, until the wheel and the clay blurred in the smoky room. Granmyr closed her eyes and put her hands upon the clay. It came suddenly to life, grew, collapsed in on itself, and gave birth to new shapes.

Kaeldra moved near, watched the clay form and

collapse and re-form like some living thing. Once, she thought she saw Myrrathog, a mountain to the east; but it melted and merged before she could be sure.

An egg grew up out of the clay, grew until it engulfed the wheel. It turned hard and smooth as a stream-polished stone.

The egg shattered. Sharp creatures jumped up out of it, tumbled, writhed, coiled.

Kaeldra heard Ryfenn's gasp of indrawn breath.

"A birthing," Granmyr whispered.

She opened her eyes, and the wheel began to slow. The creatures sank down into the egg, and then it was only a lump of clay again, soft and red-brown and ordinary. Granmyr laid her hands in her lap, and the wheel slowly slackened and stopped.

"Wha-what was that?" Ryfenn's voice was hoarse, as if it were the first time she had spoken that day.

"The Ancient Ones," Granmyr said.

She kicked the spinner with her booted foot, and it began to turn in the opposite direction. A smooth, grooved dome rose beneath her hands. She touched two fingers to the top and the dome hollowed out, became a bowl, an ordinary bowl.

"The Ancient Ones?" Ryfenn breathed. "You can't mean—but they've been gone these many years."

Granmyr stopped the wheel, stretched the cutting thread between her hands and pulled it beneath the bowl base. She set the bowl to dry with the others on the plank, then looked up at Ryfenn.

"I do mean it," Granmyr said. "The Ancient Ones. Dragons."

chapter 3

In the old times there flew into the hills of Elythia
two dragons. A storm arose; they sought shelter in a
mountain cave. The dam, being heavy with eggs,
there laid her clutch. Yet finding a village of men too
near, the dragons flew on, to return at the hatching, a
century hence. And ever after the village was called
Wyrmward, Shelter of Dragons.

—Elythian legend

Lyf slept.

All that day and the next she slept. Sometimes it
was a peaceful sleep, eyes closed, chest rising and falling
in a smooth sleep rhythm. Other times it was a feverish
sleep, when Lyf, open eyed, sat propped against a haycock
and stared right *through* Kaeldra. Then Kaeldra made
funny faces, tickled Lyf's ribs to make her laugh and come
back. Once or twice Lyf smiled, but more often she
seemed lost in a place deep inside herself.

Granmyr rummaged through her medicines, yellow-
root and ringboll and tinewort. She mashed them into
broths and pastes in a small stone bowl. The smell of
them prickled and clung inside Kaeldra's nose. Ryfenn

held Lyf in her arms as Granmyr tried to feed her. The pastes, pushed by Lyf's tongue, oozed out the corners of her mouth. The broths dribbled down her chin.

Now and again Granmyr said strange words over Lyf, half-spoken, half-sung. Often she touched two fingers to Lyf's forehead, as if hollowing the center of a pot.

Lyf slept.

Women drifted in and out of the house, neighbor women and women from the nearby village of Wyrmward. They spoke in hushed voices. They encircled Ryfenn, who sat holding Lyf and rocked and moaned.

At times, when Kaeldra came in from tending sheep, she stood outside the circle and listened to the women's talk. The war party, they said, had been victorious. The men had driven the evil thing from the mountains; although what it was, and who had seen it, varied by the teller. A few, casting eyes at Granmyr, whispered of dragons.

Once, when Kaeldra came in from the graze, the women near Ryfenn looked up quickly, startled into silence. Warming her hands by the fire, Kaeldra felt the weight of their gaze upon her. Then Granmyr strode into the house, and the women scattered like a flock of birds from a cast stone.

Wynn Calyff came to mend the roof and the clayhouse; yet when he had done, Granmyr did not move her wheel from the cottage. Then Wynn discovered a multitude of chores that needed doing. He examined the cage of Granmyr's seabird, which had disappeared mysteriously after the storm; he found nothing amiss. He repaired a wobbly stool and silenced a creaking door hinge. Mirym tagged along like a duckling who has mistaken a man for her mother.

Still Lyf slept.

"Granmyr. When will Lyf get better?"

It was three quarter-moons since the storm. Granmyr had sent Ryfenn to her cot to rest. Kaeldra tilted Lyf upright in her arms, watched the candlelight spill across her face, illuminating the dread flower-shaped rash high on one cheekbone.

Granmyr held a cup to Lyf's lips.

"Drink," Granmyr said.

Lyf's eyes stared dull ahead at nothing. Of late, she had refused even the honey gruel Ryfenn fed her.

Slowly, Granmyr poured in the broth. It pooled inside Lyf's mouth, then trickled out, ran down her chin.

Silence sat in the room like an enemy whom only Granmyr's words could drive out. Soon, she must say it. Lyf will be better soon.

The hearth fire flared and popped. Granmyr did not speak.

"Granmyr," Kaeldra said at last. "She *will* get well?"

Granmyr turned to face Kaeldra. Her eyes, in the flickering light, held a sorrow Kaeldra had never seen there before.

"I think not, child."

Panic beat its hard wings inside Kaeldra's rib cage. "But she *has* to get well. Make another potion. You must know something you can do. You *have* to make her well."

Granmyr touched Kaeldra's shoulder. "I have done all I can, child. I know no more."

Kaeldra tore Granmyr's hand away. "*Do* something. You know how, you're just not doing it. You don't care about Lyf or you'd do something to save her. You can do anything, you—"

Kaeldra buried her head in Lyf's chest. She felt the strange stillness of Lyf's body—Lyf, who usually squirmed and wiggled so hard that Kaeldra nearly dropped her. She saw the strange stillness in Lyf's eyes—Lyf, who always brimmed with mischief or wonder or joy or tears.

"Child, child . . ." Granmyr was saying. And then Kaeldra was in Granmyr's arms, and Lyf was between them, the butter between the breads as Lyf always said when Kaeldra and Mirym played the hugging game with her.

My little butter. Get better, little butter.

Granmyr's hand stroked Kaeldra's back and shoulders. Kaeldra squeezed her tight and felt for the first time how small Granmyr was, how small and frail and light.

Kaeldra pulled away. "You must—you must know something you can do?"

Granmyr's fingertips stroked her cheeks. There was a coolness where the tears smeared across her face. Granmyr shook her head.

"But I thought—"

"I know, my child. You thought I had powerful magic. But my spells are spells of knowing, not of changing. And the years have worn away most of what poor power I once possessed."

"Is there nothing you can do? Nothing?"

Granmyr turned toward the fire, as if weighing two stones in her mind, one against the other.

"There *is* something. Oh, Granmyr, what is it? Tell me what you can do."

A sudden draft stirred in the room; the candle guttered and nearly went out. Granmyr turned again toward Kaeldra. "Child," she said gently, "I am powerless against this thing. Lyf is stricken with vermilion fever. You know that."

Kaeldra knew. Rhyl Jaffyg had had vermilion fever two winters ago, and Styffa Gryeg, the winter before that. Both were vermilion-marked: a red rash, high on one cheek, shaped like a tiny vermilion blossom. Both had died in the spring.

"No medicine of mine is a match for it," Granmyr said. "There is," she hesitated, "there is but one hope, and it would be cruelty to hold it out to you."

"Granmyr, what? What is it?"

Granmyr sighed. "Against my better judgment I will show you. But you must promise not to tell anyone what you see here tonight."

"I promise. Oh, I promise. I'll never tell."

Kaeldra laid Lyf in the straw, tucked the woolen blankets around her. She followed Granmyr and sat on a milking stool by the wheel. The old woman scooped out a lump of red clay. She wedged it, thumped it on the wheel, and moistened it with water from a bowl. The wheel began to turn. It turned, Kaeldra saw, not in its usual direction, but the other way, the way it had when Granmyr worked dragons in the clay.

19

The clay rose at once to form a jagged peak, one Kaeldra did not know; it was not one of the mountains that lined the eastern sky. It spun faster, blurred, softened, and there was a thing moving low on the mountain. Two things: a man and a woman, toiling up. In the man's arms, something hung limp.

Kaeldra leaned closer, to see.

It was a child.

Fingers pressed down, and the mountain hollowed into a bowl, with the child curled inside. There was a burning in Kaeldra's head, a numbing in her limbs. The room tilted, swayed, slipped away into darkness; only the clay remained, merging, shifting, growing until it filled her eyes with other eyes: dragon eyes.

The dragon regarded her solemnly. It stretched and rolled onto its side. Its belly felt pleasant: leathery and soft. Kaeldra rubbed her cheek against it and something cool was streaming into her mouth, down her throat. It flowed out from the center of her until every part of her felt cool and good, to the tips of her fingers and toes.

"Kaeldra," the dragon said.

Kaeldra blinked.

"Kaeldra."

Granmyr was standing over her. The room was dark, the claywheel still, the fire burning low.

"What—" Kaeldra rubbed her eyes. She was sitting, as before, on the stool beside the wheel. "What happened?"

"You visioned."

"Didn't you—didn't you see it, too? It was made of clay. You made it in the clay."

"Some of it. The mountain and something moving up its side. But you watched long after the wheel had stilled."

Kaeldra shook her head to clear it. Her heart thumped in her chest; her hands felt cold. "There was a child—and a dragon. And something cool to drink."

Granmyr nodded. "Kara. As I thought."

"Kara? Who is Kara?"

"Kara was—" Granmyr sighed. She pulled up another stool and perched on it near Kaeldra. "Time it is you knew.

"Long ago," Granmyr began, "when I was a girl, I dwelt for a time among the Krags. My father had some small skill at healing; the Kragish king summoned him to ply his art upon an ailing prince.

"In those days the Ancient Ones still roamed the earth. Often and again I heard tell of some fierce, blazing battle between a dragon and men. Yet even in those days dragons seldom prevailed. Their numbers dwindled; they retreated into the mountains and ventured out to hunt only at night.

"Then came the day when Kara-of-the-Green-Eyes, Kara Dragon-sayer, summoned the kyn of dragons to the council bluff."

Granmyr's eyes, unfocused, seemed to see into another time. "Never will I forget—" She shook herself and continued.

"They call it the Migration, that day when the Ancient Ones took wing from the council bluff at Rog and soared across the Northern Sea. And afterward, King Orrik erected a fastness there and created an army of Sentinels to guard against the dragons' return. To this day the Sentinels school their troops in dragonslaying. The ancient enmity dies hard," Granmyr mused, "even when the need for it is past."

"Are they really gone?" Kaeldra asked. "No dragons have returned?"

"I have heard tales of dragon sightings, yet I credit them not. The battles are ended; the dragonpod blooms gone. Yet often have I wondered: What will befall their eggs? Dragons live, they say, for millennia; their eggs must ripen for a hundred years. The hatchings occur in cycles: a spate of hatchings over several years' time, then none for a very long time, until the next hatching cycle begins.

"A few eggs at least must have remained in the Suderlands after the Migration. Long have I listened for a hatching wind, and a dragon dam's return."

Kaeldra shivered, remembering the storm and the voices, the hatching Granmyr had worked in the clay. "But why do you tell me this? What has this to do with Lyf?"

"Kara, it is said, is the only person to survive vermilion fever. When she was a babe, her parents left her for dead entombed in a mountain cave. A moon-turn later she walked whole and hale into a village, unchanged save that her eyes had turned green. In her sleep she spoke of dragon's milk."

22

"Dragon's milk!"

"So it is said."

Kaeldra stared into the fire, tried to still her leaping thoughts. Kara. Vermilion fever. Clay eggs that hatched out dragons.

There was a rustling of hay, a soft moan.

Lyf.

"You're saying Kara was cured by—dragon's milk?"

Granmyr nodded.

"And when you worked the clay after the storm, I thought I recognized Myrrathog. And there was a birthing. A birthing, you said, of dragons."

"Yes."

"Granmyr! There must be dragons on Myrrathog! A mother, and young—and dragon's milk."

Kaeldra jumped up. "We could take Lyf. We could find the den and leave her there, like Kara."

But Granmyr was shaking her head. "Dragons are not known for their generosity to people," she said dryly. "Perhaps Kara's dragon had lost her brood and needed relief. To leave Lyf in a den with a dragon and live young—she would only die more quickly."

"Well, then what—how could we—" Kaeldra stopped, struck by an idea. "Someone could milk her. Someone—" She cast about for the someone. Granmyr was too old for climbing mountains. And Ryfenn—Ryfenn feared even the sun lizards that basked on rocks in summer. Mirym? Too young. Too clutterbrained.

"Someone," she whispered.

"Kaeldra," Granmyr said softly. "Kara was your

23

mother's mother's mother. It is believed that her descendants, those with green eyes like yours, may be dragon-sayers as well."

A shock passed through Kaeldra like a current of icy water. Her glance strayed past the fire, to Lyf.

Lyf slept.

chapter 4

And sith the sire-drake be scarlet-hued, he dare not
tarry in the lands held by men, but must hie him
away when the clutch is hatched.

—*The Bok of Dragon*

Softly, Kaeldra pulled the door shut behind her. The
dawn air splashed cold across her cheeks. Dark and sharp
against the pale streak on the horizon, the mountains
loomed.

She drank in a deep breath and set off across the
graze.

There was far to go.

Kaeldra's head felt muzzy from too little sleep. But
the cold of the air and the stretch of her legs and the
crisp, rhythmic thud of her boots sent energy surging
through her. Soon she had passed the boggy patch near
the brook; soon after, the copse of creaking blackwood

lay behind, and she had reached the standing stones atop the first rise.

The pale streak leaked across the sky. The sun rose. Underfoot, the stiff grasses gave way to rock and bracken crusted with snow. As she walked, the earth tumbled away to the west, hill and bog and ridge. And to the east, where she must go, Myrrathog. Snow clad, it blotted out all but the edges of sky.

Kaeldra, looking at the mountain, felt a tightening in her chest.

Last night Granmyr had spoken further of Kara, how she understood the language of dragons and could make known to them her thoughts. "Kara's gift," Granmyr called it. Yet Kaeldra devoutly wished to renounce kinship with this *farin* woman and revoke all claim to her terrifying gift.

Still, only with the gift might Kaeldra barter for milk to save Lyf. If she possessed it not . . .

Kaeldra recalled the heat of Lyf's cheek against hers that morning. She stopped to strap on her shoe-baskets, since the snow was deepening, and set off again.

For long hours, Kaeldra climbed. The ground steepened. Her feet numbed. The mountain was so big. From a distance it had looked smaller, flatter. It had seemed an easy thing, to find a cave large enough for dragons. But once upon it she found gorges and hillocks and precipices, and when it began to snow she knew she had no idea where to go.

Kaeldra's shoe-baskets dragged to a stop. What if I can't find the dragons? she thought. What if there are no dragons?

She stood, unable to make herself move, and the snow sifted down. The hush was so deep, Kaeldra felt she could almost hear the snowflakes as they lit.

There was a rumbling in her ears.

It was a slight trembling, which seemed to emanate from the rock, as if the mountain itself were snoring.

Kaeldra turned her head to divine its source. She could sense it now, somewhere to her left. Her shoe-baskets began to move, and the rumbling grew until it purred in her mind like a cat. As she crested a small ridge, Kaeldra blinked.

Things were growing. Ferns and mosses and even lysselblossoms, in the midst of the snow. Kaeldra shut her eyes and opened them again, but they were still there; she had not imagined them. Water dripped from nearby fir trees and beaded on the greenery, which clustered around a high rock face. Kaeldra drew near and saw that some of the rock was not rock at all, but a hole, the mouth of a cave.

She took off her shoe-baskets, then tiptoed closer, her heart pounding. She peered inside the cave, then caught her breath. It was enormous, much bigger than it had appeared from outside. The floor sloped steeply down into a cavern as tall as a needlecone tree. At the far end, the cave narrowed and was lost in shadow.

It was empty. At least, she could see nothing there, save for boulders and broken rocks and a sand-and-gravel track that wound down through the half-lit gloom. Yet the rumble continued, seeming to come from the shadowy regions deep inside.

Legs quaking, Kaeldra ventured down the track.

Warm. It was warm inside, much warmer than it ought to have been, even in the shelter of a cave. She smelled smoke and damp and a whiff of something else: a strange, scorched scent she could not identify.

One knee suddenly buckled; Kaeldra slipped. Gravel clattered down the slope, echoed against the cave walls.

When she had pulled herself to her feet, it was quiet. The rumble had stopped.

Deep inside the cave, something shifted. Something was coming, coming her way. Kaeldra shot a panicked glance back at the cave mouth. It looked small and far away. She threw herself behind a boulder and sensed a nudge at her mind, as if someone were feeling around inside her, questing, probing.

She heard it coming, or thought she heard, through the bloodbeat in her ears, a dragging sound, a scraping of something on sand. She curled herself into a tight ball.

The scorched smell thickened, filled her lungs. Sweat trickled down her forehead into her eyes. A hot wind stirred her hair.

As if drawn by some force outside herself, Kaeldra looked up.

Into an eye. It was as long as her forearm. It glowed green, corner to corner, but for a single black slit at its center.

⟨Give me your name.⟩

Kaeldra cried out as pain drove like a shaft through her skull.

The pain ebbed. Kaeldra, stunned, held her head

in her hands. The words throbbed in her mind as if seared there. Then the pain again:

⟨Give me your—⟩

"Kaeldra!"

She felt her name being drawn from her, turned over and over, as a woman handles a pot she would buy. She raised her head, and the cavern was full of scales, glinting green in the murk. Her eyes found the shape of the dragon, taller than a cottage, trailing off down the cave's curving passage.

⟨Why come you here? I know of no Kaeldra.⟩

Kaeldra held her head, waited for the throbbing to subside.

"For—" Kaeldra's throat felt dry. She swallowed. "For milk. I need dragon's milk."

⟨Milk!⟩ Blue flame roared past Kaeldra's cheek; the heat blast crested over her. ⟨You came here—for my *milk?*⟩

Kaeldra, choking on the rising smoke, scrambled backward to take refuge behind a pile of boulders. She's the mother, she thought.

"My sister needs it, my second-sister, Lyf. She is taken with vermilion fever. She will die if she doesn't get it. Here." Kaeldra fumbled with the ties on her blanket roll. She shook out its contents on the track. Three small rye cakes Ryfenn had made yesterday. A length of woolen cloth. Five leather pouches of herbs and medicines. A wedge of cheese. A carved wooden box Granmyr had given her when she was a child.

The dragon's massive head swiveled round. She

trained her eyes on the offerings. Kaeldra smelled her smoky breath, saw the throb of pulse beneath her jaw.

The dragon spat out a lick of fire; Kaeldra's things burst into flame like tinder.

⟨Rubbish.⟩

Kaeldra worked her way back through the smoke to another stand of rocks. Desperate, she slipped her amulet's leather thong over her head. "Here," she said, holding it out. "It's the most precious thing I own. My granmyr gave it to me when I was little, it is copper wrought, it—"

The dragon moved her head to it, not a foot's breadth from Kaeldra's trembling hand. Kaeldra dared not breathe.

The dragon snorted, spraying her with sparks.

Kaeldra's hand jerked back; the amulet clattered down through a chink between the rocks.

⟨Not enough!⟩

"Then what—" Kaeldra's voice came out in a croak. Her mouth felt parched; she licked her lips. "What would you like?" she whispered.

The dragon snorted again; sparks streaked through the cavern. ⟨Nothing you could give. Although I might have let you go, had you brought a lamb. I need meat, but cannot hunt. I dare not leave them alone.⟩ The dragon turned toward the cave opening, and Kaeldra felt a yearning waft, like a were-wind, through her mind.

The dragon cocked an eye at her. ⟨So *you* will have to do.⟩

The dragon's chest began to swell. She arched her

neck and sucked in through her nostrils. Sand swirled toward the dragon; Kaeldra's cloak flapped in the rush of air.

She's going to flame, Kaeldra realized. She's going to flame at me.

Kaeldra ran. She ran toward the dragon, into the dark, for she knew she could not escape by running the other way. There was a roar behind her; a blistering blast of heat. She ran past the dragon's huge claws, beside her ridged tail. She ran deep into the cave. The tail, endlessly long, began to slither backward through the passage.

The dragon was turning around.

Kaeldra ran.

Darkness thickened around her, and soon she could not see. The ground felt smooth and sandy beneath her boots; she stumbled on, feeling her way along the cave's rough walls.

Behind her, Kaeldra heard breathing and the hiss of scale on sand. She felt, rather than saw, a narrowing of the passage around her. Perhaps it would become too narrow for the dragon to follow. Perhaps there was another way out.

But the wall turned abruptly and a faint gray light illuminated a second cavern, nearly as large as the first. Snowflakes, stirred by a draft of cold air, sifted down through an opening in the cave roof. Kaeldra ran toward the hole, hoping to find some way out. Her foot thunked into something soft and she fell, sprawled out on the ground. The cave walls lit up blue. She heard a roar, and beneath it, something else, something squeaking.

The dragon stood over her. Her eyes, beneath fierce ridges, glared green.

Something soft nudged Kaeldra's cheek. Another something crept onto her back. There were soft leathery *things* all over her, nestling, clinging.

And suddenly Kaeldra knew what they were.

Dragons. Baby dragons.

chapter 5

Bargain not with a dragon.

—*Dragonslayer's Guyde*

⟨Get away from my draclings.⟩

The words spilled inside Kaeldra's head like scalding water. Nostrils flaring, the dragon spewed out sparks.

Kaeldra scooted backward, her head throbbing, the stench of dragon breath burning her lungs. The dragon wouldn't flame now, not with the draclings so near, clinging to her. They were her protection.

⟨Get away from my draclings!⟩

I need milk, Kaeldra tried to say, but the words stuck in her throat; no sound came out.

The dragon flamed in rage above her. The cavern lit up blue, then dimmed to smoky gray. A gnarled claw, its talons long as daggers, lifted off the ground and hovered over Kaeldra. She pressed her body into the cold sand. There was a ripping of cloth, and a smooth shaft slid across her skin. Her tunic tightened around her chest. The ground dropped. She was hanging in midair.

"Watch the babies!" she cried. They were slipping away. Her protection was slipping away.

She felt them peel off her, one by one, heard the soft thuds as they hit the sand. Then she was hurtling through the air, slamming into the ground. She pulled herself to her hands and knees, gasping, spitting out sand, struggling to collect the strands of an idea.

Watch the babies.

What was it the dragon had said? *I need meat, but cannot hunt. I dare not leave them alone.*

"I could watch your babies," Kaeldra said.

The dragon advanced, swiveling her head to fix Kaeldra with glowering green eyes. Kaeldra crawled backward toward the deep shadows at the rear of the cavern, not daring to turn away from those eyes. Perhaps there was a passage, another way out.

"You could hunt. I would watch them. I'm good with babies. I take care of my second-sister, Lyf, all the time. She's the one who needs the milk, my second-sister, Lyf."

Kaeldra's foot hit a rock. She scrambled back around it. The dragon followed, all scales and claws and teeth. Kaeldra glimpsed an indentation in the cave wall, back and to the right. A passage?

"You could stay out all night—I don't mind. I'll

keep them safe. I know how to scare away wolves and holt cats. I care for our sheep."

The dragon glared, her green eyes luminescent in the gloom. She was so close, Kaeldra could have touched her, so close her breath scorched Kaeldra's skin.

It's no use, Kaeldra thought. Her idea hadn't worked.

She lunged for the passage. The dragon flamed. Fire licked against the darkness; Kaeldra screamed and slammed against the cavern wall. Not a passage. A dead end. She crouched, staring up at the dragon, waiting for the heat blast she knew would come.

The eyes blinked and looked away.

The yearning again. It blew into her mind as the dragon turned toward the cave mouth. Then the dragon whipped her head back toward Kaeldra.

⟨If harm befalls them, I will know it. I will find you and make you pay.⟩

"It won't. I promise. I'll care for them as if they were mine."

Kaeldra sensed a turmoil behind the dragon eyes, a stirring and pitching of alien emotions. Then, slowly, the dragon turned away. Scratching at the sand, she uncovered a pile of large, smooth stones and flamed at them; they glowed as if struck by blue lightning. The dragon covered the stones with sand. She nudged her babies near the warm place, flicking at them with her long forked tongue, making whiffling noises with her nose.

⟨I will return at dawn,⟩ the dragon said. ⟨See that

you are here. Keep them warm, and do not allow them outside.⟩ She hesitated. ⟨If there is trouble, call for me. Call Fiora, and I will come.⟩

And she passed out of the cavern, a glittering procession of neck and back and tail, awesome in its immensity, surprising in its grace.

Kaeldra crouched on the sand, taking deep gulps of smoky air. Better go now. Better run. Better run away, run home and never come back.

But she would find me. *See that you are here,* she had said. *I will find you and make you pay.*

And I understood her, Kaeldra thought. I *am* a dragon-sayer. But she took little comfort from the fact, for she knew how near she had come to death.

Kaeldra breathed long and deep until her mind began to settle. It settled around the thought of Lyf, Lyf drinking the milk, Lyf opening her eyes and seeing, really seeing.

And Kaeldra knew she had to stay.

It was growing dark. Only a thin, gray light trickled down from the opening in the roof.

The draclings were huddled together in a lumpy pile, which expanded and collapsed as they breathed.

Were they asleep?

Kaeldra hoped so. It was true, as she had told Fiora, that she was good with children. She was good with lambs, too, and piglets, and kids.

But these—these were *dragons.*

Kaeldra tiptoed to where they lay. Wary, she knelt beside them. In the dim light she could see that there were three of them, each the size of a large puppy or a byre cat full grown. Two of the draclings' heads were hidden beneath a leg or a tail, so Kaeldra could not tell for certain whether they were asleep. The third one's eyes were squeezed shut.

Kaeldra reached out to touch it. The dracling squeaked, jerked up its head, and stared at her through the bluish film that covered its eyes.

Kaeldra froze. Would it bite her? Would it flame?

The dracling let out a tiny snort, then squirmed deeper into the pile.

Kaeldra watched for a moment. They seemed to be sleeping. Tentatively, she brushed a finger across one of the draclings' sides. Its yellow-tan skin was wrinkled and loose. It felt powdery, like butterfly wings.

She stroked the dracling's sides, fingered the leathery ridge that ran down its neck and back. Its skin looked translucent, like her own wrists where the veins showed through. It was hard to see clearly in the dim light, but this one—the largest—seemed to have a reddish cast; the others were tinged with green.

Kaeldra's hand slid over the largest dracling's side and felt something hard, like the horn buds on a goat kid's head. Horns? Growing out of its sides? She tried to picture Fiora's sides. Scales and scales and—something else, something fluttery. Wings. These were wing buds.

The dracling exhaled and whistled softly, an oddly contented sound. Kaeldra felt a rush of tenderness. They were babies, only babies, after all.

Darkness pressed in close. There was a candle in her

blanket roll, and flint and iron. They were still in the outer cavern, if they had not been burned. Kaeldra checked the draclings—still sleeping—then groped back the way she had come along the hard, bumpy walls of the passage. At last the passage widened, and far away, she saw stars in a deep night sky. The snow had stopped.

After much searching, she found her blanket roll. The candle had melted a little, but since it had lain on its side, it was not too misshapen to use. Kaeldra struck a spark and blew until it caught. She lit the candle and examined the earthenware jar she had brought for the milk. It was unbroken. Then Kaeldra remembered something else.

Her amulet. She had to find her amulet.

She retraced her way along the track until her candlelight spilled across the charred place in the sand. Nearby were the rocks between which her amulet had fallen. Kaeldra pulled at them. They were big, impossible to move. She moved her candle over the rocks. Even in the light, the spaces between them were black. Kaeldra jammed her hand into chink after chink until it was scratched and bloody. At last, she was forced to give up.

Her amulet was gone.

> Lose your amulet 'fore granted,
> Future husband you've recanted.

The old wives' warning rang through her mind. Instinctively, Kaeldra clutched at the place where her amulet had always been.

38

What difference does it make? she thought. No one would have me anyway. Especially now. Ryfenn was right: I don't belong. I am a dragon-sayer and therefore doubly *farin*.

Slowly, she walked back to the inner cavern.

In the light-circle hollowed out by her candle, she could see that the draclings were still sleeping. She bent down and stroked one. It stirred, then stumbled over its siblings like a newborn puppy, making little smacking sounds with its mouth.

Kaeldra dug the end of her candle into the sand and leaned against a boulder. She unstoppered her waterskin and soaked a corner of her gown, then held the dripping cloth over her lap. The dracling clambered onto her, snuffling, until it found the cloth. It began to suck. Its breath whistled softly. It kneaded Kaeldra's legs with its talons.

Kaeldra ran her hand along the dracling's side. Her eyelids felt heavy, and a peacefulness came over her. The stone heat seeped into her bones.

She didn't know what woke her.

Sunshine poured in through the roof hole. Kaeldra shivered. A cold draft played about her hair. Something, some *things* were heaped in her lap.

Draclings.

Still sleeping, they felt surprisingly light. Kaeldra laughed softly, stroked them one by one.

A twinge of pain stung her head. Kaeldra looked up. Her heart lurched.

Fiora, the mother dragon, was staring down at her. ⟨Go now.⟩

Kaeldra lifted a sleeping dracling off her lap. She started to remove another one, then hesitated, remembering. "What about the milk?" she asked.

⟨What about it?⟩

"You promised. That was our bargain. I would watch your babies, and you would give me milk."

⟨I promised no milk.⟩

Kaeldra stared at the dragon. Yes, she had! She had said she'd give her milk! Or—had she? Kaeldra thought back to the night before, tried to remember Fiora's words.

If harm befalls them, I will know it. I will return at dawn. See that you are here.

Fiora had never promised milk. She hadn't promised anything. Kaeldra only thought she had.

She had failed. She had tried to bargain with a dragon and she had failed. Kaeldra bit her lip; tears sprang to her eyes.

⟨Oh, very well. Take your milk.⟩ Fiora lowered herself to the ground and lay on her side. The length of her—body, neck and tail—encircled the cavern.

Astonished, Kaeldra nudged the two remaining draclings from her lap. She rushed to get the jar from her blanket roll before Fiora could change her mind. But Fiora lay still, looking sleepy and sated. Kaeldra fumbled with her blanket, feeling vaguely unsettled. That was easy. Too easy.

The little ones stirred. One by one they opened their eyes and began to squeak. The reddish one tottered toward its mother; there was a sudden rush of draclings for teats. Kaeldra hastened to claim one. She uncorked her jar and set it down, unsure how to begin.

The dragon had two rows of teats along her belly, which was soft and yellow hued, like tanned leather. Kaeldra chose a teat and positioned her jar in the sand beneath it. At that moment, one of the draclings lunged, knocking down the jar.

Kaeldra gave the dracling a gentle shove; it slithered away, squeaking. She glanced up at Fiora, hoping she hadn't seen. The dragon, eyes hooded, regarded her mockingly.

Kaeldra set up her jar again and soon jets of blue milk were splashing into it in a regular rhythm. It wasn't much different from milking a cow or a goat. The hardest part, she found, was fending off the draclings. In an orgy of feeding, they guzzled at teat after teat, often leaping at Kaeldra's stream of milk. She hunched over her jar to keep them away.

Suddenly, one of the draclings was hurtling between Kaeldra's arms. It landed in front of her, toppling the jar. Blue milk seeped into the sand. Kaeldra grabbed for the jar, but too late.

The milk was gone.

⟨There goes your milk.⟩ The dragon cocked an eye at Kaeldra. Did she plan this? Kaeldra wondered.

"But—but Lyf. But I need—"

⟨More? Indeed you do. But how will you pay for it?⟩

"Pay for it? I don't know, I—"

⟨Take your milk. But you owe me. In a half-moon

41

I will expect payment. You will return and care for my draclings, as you did this past night.⟩

"But I can't—"

⟨Very well, then. Good-bye.⟩ The dragon shut her eyes.

"But—"

Fiora's eyes flew open. She cocked her head and glared down at Kaeldra. *It's not fair*, Kaeldra thought. *She tricked me. How will I get away again? Just let me get home, get the milk to Lyf, make her better. Maybe the dragon will forget. She can't* make *me come back.*

A bolt of pain ripped through her head.

⟨Don't tempt me.⟩ Fiora narrowed her long, green eyes. ⟨I will find you and make you pay.⟩

chapter 6

I send this boy, my aide; for there is a traitor among
the brethren, I know not who. Tell the boy nothing;
he is innocent of this. Send him back when he is fed
and well-rested. When I can, I will dispatch another
to help. Wait and be wary. Keep the girl close.

—Letter to Granmyr,
Landerath

𝕾he's here!"

Mirym unbent and ran to Kaeldra. "Did you get it?"

Kaeldra stepped inside, breathing in the familiar
home smells: wood smoke, herbs, damp feathers, a lingering of soup. Granmyr and Ryfenn, hunched over
something near the fire, looked up.

Kaeldra nodded.

"Oh, Kael!" Mirym grabbed Kaeldra's hand, dragged
her toward Granmyr and Ryfenn and a rounded form
covered by blankets. A sudden, choking feeling gripped
her. "Am I too late? Is she—?"

Granmyr bolted up and fumbled through Kaeldra's

43

blanket roll. Firelight flared across the form as Ryfenn took it in her lap. It was Lyf. She lay stiller than Kaeldra had ever seen her, so still she could not see her breathe. "Is she—?" Kaeldra said again.

Granmyr funneled the milk into a waterskin and knelt by Lyf. Gently, she squeezed the skin. A little milk squirted out in a blue thread, quivered on Lyf's lips, trickled down her cheek.

Granmyr struck her knee with a clenched fist, made a harsh sound in her throat. Ryfenn sobbed.

One drop still trembled on Lyf's mouth, glistened blue in the firelight. Lyf's lips moved slightly. Kaeldra thought at first that she had imagined it. Yet the drop slid in.

"Look," Kaeldra breathed.

Lyf stirred. She licked her lips.

Granmyr squeezed the skin, and Kaeldra saw the swallowing in Lyf's throat. Shadows flickered across her cheeks as they hollowed and filled, hollowed and filled. A great happiness surged through Kaeldra. Granmyr, turning to Kaeldra, her voice hoarse, said, "It's taking."

"It's taking! It's taking!" Mirym sang.

Lyf drank, drank until the waterskin was half-empty. Then she slowed; her mouth slackened. Granmyr put down the skin. Lyf's chest rose and fell. A smile touched the corners of her mouth.

Lyf slept.

Ryfenn laid the child in the straw, and then Granmyr was taking Kaeldra's blanket roll, and Mirym was taking her cloak. Ryfenn went to the stew pot and came back with a steaming bowl of soup. Mirym set a stool by the fire and motioned Kaeldra to sit.

"Tell me what happened, Kael," Mirym said, unlacing one of Kaeldra's boots. "Did the medicine woman give it to you or did you have to steal it?"

"What med—?"

Granmyr cleared her throat.

Kaeldra looked up quickly and met Granmyr's glance. She gulped a spoonful of soup, burning her mouth. "Oh, the medicine woman," Kaeldra said. "She, uh, gave it to me."

"What is it? It looks like milk, only it's *blue*."

"It—it is milk, only—"

"She must have put a spell on it," Granmyr said.

"Yes. Yes, she did. She—put a spell on it and turned it blue," Kaeldra said. She scooted back from the fire a bit, feeling suddenly warm, too warm.

Ryfenn, stirring the soup, pursed her lips.

"Oh," Mirym said. "I can't wait to tell Wynn." Mirym pulled off one boot and started unlacing the other. "So she gave it to you? That's all? Granmyr said she's tricky."

"Uh, well." Kaeldra swallowed again. She wished Mirym would stop asking questions. She didn't know what Granmyr wanted her to say. Then she remembered something, something she'd have to explain. "My amulet. I gave her my amulet."

Mirym sat back on her heels and stared, round eyed. Granmyr's head jerked up. Ryfenn dropped the ladle into the soup.

45

"I had to," Kaeldra said. "That was the only way she'd give me the milk."

"But now you can never—" Mirym looked horrified. Then she was hugging her. "Oh, Kael," Mirym said. "You're so good. Oh, Kael."

Ryfenn walked to Lyf, looked down at the sleeping child. She turned to Kaeldra. "Thank you," Ryfenn whispered.

The warmth of the soup and the warmth of the fire flowed into Kaeldra, made her feel good, better than she could remember ever feeling. *Thank you. Ryfenn said thank you.*

Kaeldra's spoon scraped the bottom of her bowl and Ryfenn was there, taking it from her. Steam twined, merged with the fire smoke as Ryfenn ladled more soup into her bowl. Ryfenn serving *her*. Ryfenn acting as if she were someone special.

There was a knock at the door.

Kaeldra jumped. Ryfenn stopped the ladle halfway between pot and bowl; soup dripped, steaming, onto the rushes.

"I'll get it," Mirym said.

"No," Granmyr said. "I will."

It was a youth. He could not have been much older than Kaeldra, yet he was taller than anyone she knew; the top of his head grazed the lintel.

The young man reached inside his cloak and handed something to Granmyr. She looked up sharply. Kaeldra heard the murmur of their voices as Granmyr fingered the thing he had given her. A bird fluttered on his wrist:

a gyrfalcon, hooded. He stroked it gently with a massive hand; the bird quieted.

Granmyr returned the thing she had held. The youth ducked and stepped into the room. As he moved out of the shadows into the firelight, Kaeldra caught her breath. His hair was the color of *her* hair; his eyes, incredibly, were blue.

"This is Jeorg Sigrad," Granmyr said, taking his cloak, which draped in folds of vibrant scarlet—unheard of in Elythia. "He is a friend of a friend and will sup with us tonight."

Granmyr introduced the family; the young man nodded, pushing back a lock of yellow hair that had fallen into his eyes. And it came to Kaeldra with a sudden shock how she must appear to the others. This youth was clearly *farin*, and he looked like her. He was tall, even taller than she, and except for the green of her eyes, their coloring was the same.

"Ryfenn," Granmyr said, "the soup?"

"But he is a Krag!" Ryfenn whispered. "You promised—"

"He is hungry. He is a friend of a friend."

Ryfenn, her mouth tight with disapproval, moved the ladle. Soup poured from it; steam swirled in the firelight. Ryfenn held out the bowl to the stranger: Kaeldra's bowl, the bowl she had been filling for Kaeldra.

"Would you care for some soup?" Ryfenn asked.

"More soup, Master Jeorg?" Mirym smiled and picked up the stranger's bowl.

47

"Oh, no, miss, I couldn't," he said, but his eyes strayed longingly toward the pot.

"Nonsense! There is plenty," Granmyr said. "We insist."

Mirym scurried to replenish his soup. He must have been hungry, Kaeldra thought. Already he had consumed three bowls of soup and two loaves of bread. Between mouthfuls he answered Granmyr's queries about the trading in Regalch, the Krags' disastrous foray into Vittongal. His courtesy never flagged, and yet there seemed to Kaeldra to be something guarded, something *careful* about this Kragish youth. He sat too carefully erect. His voice was too carefully deep.

Now Granmyr descended into the cellar and returned with a wine flask. As she poured wine into the Krag's goblet she said, "So, Master Jeorg. Landerath sent no letter."

The young man reached for his goblet and lifted it nearly to his lips before he seemed to remember himself and checked his arm.

"To the vine," Granmyr said, as a signal for all to raise their goblets.

"To the vine," the youth repeated. He sipped, and then answered carefully, "No. Only what I've told you, and his brooch. That was all."

"He says not to fear, you say. That *you* will put an end to the menace."

The Krag nodded gravely. "Yes. I will do it."

"Ah," Granmyr said, also nodding. Then she leaned forward abruptly. "And what menace is that?"

"Well, *you* know." Reddening, he glanced around

48

the table, at a loss. "The dragons, of course."

Kaeldra choked on her wine. Through the beating of her heart, she heard Ryfenn's suppressed shriek. The Krag drew himself up, and his voice, when he spoke, seemed deeper than before. "I am a dragonslayer," he said, "with the Sentinels, on Rog."

"How odd," Granmyr said. "I thought the Rogish dragonslayers all wore copper armbands."

"Oh, armbands, yes, well. You see—" He swallowed and pushed back a truant lock of hair. "I'm *almost* a dragonslayer. Officially, that is. I was going to be initiated this summer, but this was more important. The ceremony is just a formality. I'm fully trained of course, but—"

"Praise the stars you're here!" Ryfenn burst out. "I've been so worried, I can hardly sleep nights. Oh, when will you slay them? When will we know peace?"

"Ah, it shouldn't be long. Especially if you show me the place where they lair."

"Where they lair?" Ryfenn's voice came out a squeak. "But how would *we* know? You're the one to discover that."

"But Landerath said—" His eyes flicked toward Kaeldra. "I thought—"

"Who sent you?" Granmyr's voice was quiet, too quiet. "Why are you here?"

"I—I told you," the youth said, "because Landerath—" He swiped at his hair, his face now bright pink. Kaeldra, surprised at herself, almost felt sorry for him. For a long moment he and Granmyr locked eyes. The gyrfalcon, hooded and tethered to a stool, rustled its wings.

"Tell him, Granmyr!" Mirym burst out. "The storm! The portent in the clay!"

"A portent?" the Krag asked. His blue eyes broke free from Granmyr's gaze, moved to look past Mirym, past Ryfenn, at Kaeldra.

"Know you of these dragons, miss? Anything at all?"

Kaeldra heard the softening, the plea in his voice. She caught Granmyr's warning glance and was filled with confusion. She longed to tell him, at least give him a clue. If he killed Fiora—then she wouldn't have to keep her promise. She'd never have to go back to that awful place again.

Involuntarily she recalled the feel of the baby dragons: how light they were, how their sides rose and fell in sleep breathing.

"Kaeldra, the young man asked you a question." Ryfenn looked up at him from where she knelt by Lyf. "I don't know what comes over her. I try to teach her manners but," she smiled, "you know how it is. With some, it just doesn't take."

He had eaten her soup. Ryfenn had been about to give her more soup, and he had taken it. Kaeldra looked into his eyes. Blue eyes. He had blue eyes, not brown eyes like everybody else except Kaeldra. And he was tall, too, but Ryfenn didn't care. He was *farin*, but she had smiled at him, had taken his side against Kaeldra.

"*Know* you aught of this?" the Kragish youth asked again.

"No," Kaeldra said. "Nothing. Nothing at all."

chapter 7

If you would seek out dragons, seek first for a green-eyed girl.

—*Dragonslayer's Guyde*

Dragons," said the dragonslayer, "are the *sneakiest* creatures on Hort's green earth."

"Truly?" Mirym asked.

"Oh, yes." The youth reached for another seedcake. Steam from his tea twined upward, mingled with dust motes in a shaft of morning light. Lyf sat on Kaeldra's lap, drowsed against her.

"They have to be," he continued, "because they're so vulnerable."

"What! Surely, Master Jeorg, you don't mean to tell us those dreadful creatures are vulnerable," Ryfenn said, pushing a crock of corberry sweetpulp in his direction.

Last night after supper Ryfenn had bustled about, taking hay and blankets for him into the clayhouse. *That poor boy is going to slay those dragons for us,* she had said. *We can't send him out again on a night like this.*

This *farin* youth had won Ryfenn over in a few short hours, Kaeldra thought, and *she* had been trying for years.

Now he slathered his seedcake with sweetpulp and spoke between bites. "It is not widely known—except among those of us who have studied them, of course. But a dragon's underbelly is as soft as"—he looked round for an object of comparison—"as this loaf of bread. One swift jab, thusly"—he plunged his knife into the loaf—"and *pfft.* It's ended." Kaeldra winced, recalling the softness of the draclings' bellies.

"Indeed," the dragonslayer continued, "they've been known to kill themselves by accidentally dragging over a sharp rock."

"That can't be!" Mirym cried. "Otherwise we wouldn't need dragonslayers at all, we'd just—"

"Oh, well," he said, breaking the bread and spreading it with sweetpulp, "I didn't say it was easy. The problem is getting close enough for that one jab. Somehow you've got to keep them from roasting you with their breath or raking you with their claws. Their teeth are no pot of clams, either. And, as I said, they're sneaky."

"So what do you do?" Mirym asked. "It sounds hopeless."

Ryfenn poured more tea into the dragonslayer's mug. It was strange, almost amusing, Kaeldra thought, how the young man became easy of tongue before the admiring attentions of Mirym and Ryfenn. Before Granmyr had left, he had been more quiet, as if testing the impact of each word.

Strange, too, was the way Kaeldra felt drawn to him one moment and fearful the next. But, "I trust not this Master Jeorg," Granmyr had told Kaeldra late last night, "and neither should you."

"There's an art to it," he was saying now. "You have to study the lore, plan your strategy. Well, take Porphy, for example. A dragon was laying waste to the countryside near his town, oh, this was hundreds of years ago, but the story is clearly transcribed in our archives. Porphy had read all the writings on dragons, and he knew that their bellies are their most vulnerable parts. He knew also of these." The youth drew from his tunic a tiny silvery cylinder. "A single, high-pitched note will entrance them. Here, let me show you." He blew on the pipe; a shrill note pierced the air. He put away the pipe, then continued.

"Trouble is, the trance lasts only until you run out of breath. When you sound the pipe again, the dragon is alerted and will not be tranced a second time. Anyhow, Porphy found the path between the dragon's lair and its water supply, and he dug a pit. . . ."

Lyf stirred, looked up and smiled a sleepy smile. She had a clean smell to her, Kaeldra thought, a milky smell, like a newborn baby. Kaeldra closed her eyes, still weary from her journey. The Krag's voice droned on and on like a bee on a summer's day. The things he spoke of had nothing to do with Kaeldra; had no more substance than steam or light.

Between Kaeldra's arms, Lyf's body stretched with

breath; under Kaeldra's hand her heartthrob pulsed.

". . . incredibly light," he was saying. "Young dragons actually float in their sleep."

"No, they don't," Kaeldra said.

"What?" the youth asked, taken aback.

"Oh, I—" Kaeldra looked down. Why had she said that? She was supposed to be on her guard. "Nothing," she said.

Silence filled the room, thick as smoke. Kaeldra concentrated hard on Lyf's hair, smoothing it with her fingers. And then he was speaking again, of heroes and of dragons, of bravery and of guile.

Granmyr had been silent, too, last night, when Kaeldra had told her privately of the dragons. Later, Granmyr had spoken of eyes. "It is the green in your eyes," she had said, and it seemed to Kaeldra that her voice held something new, a kind of respect, mixed with sadness. "You must go back. You must not break a promise to a dragon."

But now, groping back in her mind, Kaeldra could not quite recall having made a promise. What exactly had she said? The memory had dimmed and receded until Kaeldra could almost imagine that it had been a terrible nightmare, that it had not really happened at all.

". . . a little like Kaeldra's only greener," Jeorg was saying.

"Her eyes are hazel." Granmyr stood in the doorway.

The youth started. "Ah, well, actually—" he began. "If you see them in a certain light—" He leaned forward, gazed into Kaeldra's eyes and said with sudden defiance,

"In my country they say eyes like those are dragon-sayer's eyes."

Kaeldra felt the warmth creep up her face. She wanted to look away, but couldn't, not while this young man was looking at her; she couldn't pull away from the astonishing blue of his eyes.

"We're not in your country," Granmyr snapped.

"True," the youth said, turning at last from Kaeldra. "Still," he murmured under his breath, "it's odd."

"That it is," Kaeldra heard Ryfenn say softly. "Odd, indeed."

The Krag left after breakfast. He retrieved his falcon from the clayhouse and headed across the hills toward Wyrmward on a dapple-white mare. Later that day Granmyr moved her wheel back into the clayhouse. Little by little life slipped again into its familiar pattern, except that it was lambing time, and Kaeldra stayed in the fields from daybreak until long after dusk. Lyf grew in heft and vigor every day, and the rash began to fade from her cheek.

It was easy for Kaeldra to keep the dragons a secret, for sometimes she did not quite believe in them herself. But one evening, a quarter-moon after her return, two days after the dragon's milk had run out, she came in from the fields early to find Lyf asleep.

"Ryfenn," Kaeldra asked, "did Lyf miss her nap today?"

"No. She napped."

"Look, she's asleep already."

Ryfenn put down her spoon and came to Kaeldra.

Lyf breathed softly on a blanket near the fire. "Well," Ryfenn said, "she needs her rest. She's recovering." Ryfenn went back to her cooking, but for the rest of the evening she was silent, and furrows creased her brow.

Four days later, the rash was back, sharply etched on Lyf's cheek. Now she was always sleeping when Kaeldra came home. Mirym said Lyf stayed awake all morning, but after the noon meal she lay down and did not rise until the following day.

Kaeldra stroked Lyf's face and felt a dread and a hopelessness. Fiora reared up in her mind, filled her thoughts.

"The milk was taking, Kael," Mirym said, as though trying to console her for letting them down. "It just wasn't—"

"I know. It wasn't enough."

As Lyf grew worse, Kaeldra often caught Ryfenn staring at her, as if Lyf's illness were somehow her fault. Sometimes, as Ryfenn turned away, Kaeldra thought she saw her move her thumb and little finger in the sign-against-evil. Once Kaeldra let a mug slip from her hands; it broke upon the floor.

"Isn't that just like you," Ryfenn snapped. "Breaking things, losing your amulet. Now you'll never marry, and you'll be on my hands forever."

On the fourteenth day, the day Fiora had commanded Kaeldra to return, Granmyr came to where she was tending sheep in the graze. Kaeldra watched as she picked her way up the snow-patched hillside, surrounded by a shifting tide of sheep. She sat by Kaeldra, on a boulder near the blackwood copse. "Lyf needs more milk," Granmyr said.

Kaeldra picked at the moss on the boulder. She knew it.

"When will you go?"

A newborn lamb bleated pitifully. Behind her, Kaeldra felt the shadow of the mountains stretch down and chill her back.

"I don't want to," she said.

Granmyr's hand lightly touched her own. "I know, child," she said. "But you must."

"Couldn't someone else go?"

Granmyr shook her head. "I'll say that I sent you for medicine. Mirym can tend the flock."

"I'm afraid," Kaeldra whispered.

"You are the one fate has named. Your eyes—"

"I don't care about my eyes! I wish they were brown or gray or even blue. Any color but green!"

Granmyr sighed. "Kara's gift is not an easy one to own, I grant you. Your mother—"

Kaeldra looked up. Granmyr seldom spoke of her mother. When Kaeldra had used to ask about her, Granmyr avoided answering. In time Kaeldra had come to believe that her mother had done something shameful. No one ever spoke of a father, and Kaeldra was afraid to ask.

"Your mother was forced to flee Kragrom, for the ruling powers feared her gift. They thought she possessed a wizardry that could one day overthrow them. She was the last of Kara's heirs, except, of course, for you. She was ill and knew she had not long to live. So he sent the two of you to me."

"*Who* sent us? My father?"

"No. He was killed in the wars long before. It was—Hush!" Granmyr gripped Kaeldra's hand. Then Kaeldra heard it, too, a thundering in the ground.

And a motley troop of horsemen galloped up from the valley, scattering sheep. Kaeldra jumped up to collect the flock, but Granmyr would not release her hand.

"What do you want?" Granmyr demanded of the leader, Rhyll Ilyff, the smithy. Behind him, shifting uneasily in their saddles, were men from neighboring farms and from the village of Wyrmward.

"Move aside, old woman. We would speak with the green-eyed one."

Granmyr pulled Kaeldra behind her, which was absurd, for the top of Granmyr's head came only to Kaeldra's chin. "The only eyes here are brown and hazel. Unless you would speak with sheep—"

Rhyll Ilyff leaned forward in his saddle, anger darkening his face. "That girl's eyes are green enough for our purpose."

"And what would that be?"

"You know very well, old woman. A dragon menaces the crofts of Elythia; the Kragish youth tells it. A green-eyed one could track the beast, bring us glory in place of shame. Now move aside!"

Granmyr did not budge. Rhyll Ilyff spurred his horse forward; Kaeldra grabbed Granmyr, twisted away and fell, dragging the old woman down with her. But Granmyr shook her off and rose to her feet, shouting, "You, Yan

Styval! You bounced Kaeldra on your knee when she was little more than a babe. And now you would send her to track dragons?"

Yan looked embarrassed and squirmed in his saddle. "She always was a strange one," he muttered.

"And you, Jayk Pyreth, and you, Brys Wyffad, and—Wynn Calyff! Does your mother know you're here?"

Wynn's face reddened. He did not meet Granmyr's eyes. "Yes, she—no, she—I can do what I please; I'm grown now, I don't have to ask my mother."

"Grown, are you? Come to get a young girl to do your work. And what would you do? Tie her up like a horse thief and flog her until she produces your dragon? Is this the glory of which you speak? Shame on you! Shame on you all!"

"Don't listen to the old shrew!" Rhyll Ilyff spun round and addressed the men. "We won't hurt the girl. She's got green eyes. I told you what that means. She likely knows where it is even now!"

But the others were muttering amongst themselves, casting furtive glances at Granmyr and Kaeldra. Brys Wyffad turned his horse around and headed back across the graze. Then, two and three at a time, the others followed.

"Cowards!" shouted their leader, galloping after them. "Afraid of an old woman and a girl!"

When the last faint hoofbeat had stilled, Granmyr turned to Kaeldra.

"You must go to the dragon," she said. "You must leave tonight."

chapter 8

Six pewter spoons, two sheep, one leather boot, four apples, one ox-yoke, one ox, one leather jerkin, seventeen fish, one pair linen trousers, five anchor-weight crushed limestone.

—Being the contents
of the stomach
of a dragon slain near Rog,
A Historie of Dragons

hello?"

Kaeldra's voice washed back at her from deep within the cave. She stood in the dappled light, peering into the darkness, waiting, she didn't know for what. Not a greeting, certainly. Perhaps some sign the dragons had heard her. At the very least, a sign the dragons were there.

But she knew they were there, or had been recently. She had seen the heat-shimmer above the snow; she had passed, near the cave mouth, the eruption of greenery, outlandish in a world glazed white.

Kaeldra edged inside, uneasy. It was warm, as she had remembered. Behind, she could hear the drip of meltwater on stone. Ahead, she could make out the shapes of boulders and rock heaps and the track that wound down among them into the shadows.

Kaeldra knelt and untied her blanket roll. She had better light her torch here where she could still see.

The *chink* of iron on flint echoed loudly in the cave. Now she must know I'm here, she thought. Why doesn't she do something? Kaeldra tried to imagine the dragons, far back in the second cavern. Fiora must be doing something. But what?

A spark lit on the punk; Kaeldra blew to kindle it and dropped it on the torch. She retied her blanket roll and walked with the torch down the track through the cavern and into the passage beyond, darkness creeping ever closer. Her shadow blackened, split, flared out from her feet in a quavery wedge.

A sudden smoky odor, different from the torch smell, filled her nose. Kaeldra's neck prickled. Just walk, she told herself.

A tingling sensation inside her head. Not a headache, but more like the beginning of a sneeze or the way a feather would feel if it got inside and tickled.

Kaeldra stopped. Something about that feeling, something—

Whonk! Something hurtled through the air, clawed at her shoulder, and thudded at her feet.

She screamed. Her torch slipped out of her hands. Darkness flooded in.

Something attacked the backs of her thighs, then slid to the ground.

Still screaming, Kaeldra whirled around. She ran

back the way she had come, feeling her way along the bumpy cave walls. Something pounced on her back, clung to her blanket roll. She tried to shake it off, but it stuck fast, jouncing as she ran.

A faint light ahead. The cavern. *Run!*

The cave opened up; a sudden pain stabbed at her toes. She lurched forward, slammed into the sand.

⟨Get back in there!⟩

The voice was a ripping inside Kaeldra's head. A hot wind scorched her face. Sparks streaked past, and beyond them green eyes flashed in a glittering sea of scales.

Fiora.

Kaeldra's three small attackers scurried past her into the cave. One of them was dragging her torn blanket.

The dragon watched them go, then turned to glare at Kaeldra. ⟨You're late.⟩

She had forgotten how much it hurt. The voice felt like an orange-hot ball of metal, a molten mass inside her head. The hurt was so bad, Kaeldra couldn't comprehend the words until the voice stopped and the words pulsed in her mind, an afterglow of pain.

"I—couldn't get away. I—"

⟨You're lying.⟩

Pain again. Fiora's breath-stench lay heavy in the air; Kaeldra nearly retched. She wanted to deny the lie, but felt the truth trailing toward Fiora like a draft-tugged wisp of smoke: ⟨I did not want to come.⟩

⟨Hah!⟩ Fiora snorted. ⟨But you did come. Why?⟩

"I need more milk," Kaeldra whispered.

62

⟨That wasn't our bargain! You are beholden to me!⟩ Fiora's rage flamed a jagged path through Kaeldra's head.

"I know. But Lyf will die. I need more milk."

⟨It will cost you.⟩

"I know."

The dragon turned toward the cave mouth, and Kaeldra felt again the yearning she had felt the last time she was there. She felt a buoying up, a sense of joy and flight and freedom.

Then Fiora's voice cut her off.

⟨I go now. When I return, you may have your milk. Then you will owe me anew. In a half-moon—no later— you will come. You will tend my draclings whilst I hunt.⟩

"I will," Kaeldra promised.

Fiora began to move, and Kaeldra scrambled out of her way, marveling, in spite of herself, at the lightness of the dragon's gait. Fiora fairly *pranced*, her head held high, her body swaying gently, the tips of her talons seeming hardly to touch the ground. Her wings, streaming from her shoulders, were awash in misty rainbows; her scales glimmered emerald in the gloom.

Something caught at Kaeldra's throat, and she forgot, for a moment, the pain of Fiora's voice, the sharpness of her talons, the deadly conflagration of her breath.

Fiora moved into the sun, her scales exploding with light.

Kaeldra's blanket roll had been torn off in the passage just beyond the outer cavern. She fumbled through the sand, collecting her things into a pile, barely able to see them in the gloom. The milk jar—thank the heavens—was unbroken, although the food was sandy and she could not find her flint. At last she felt it beneath a torn scrap of blanket.

She groped back through the dark passage in search of her torch, first walking and feeling for it with her feet, then scratching blindly in the cold damp sand on hands and knees. By the time she bumped into it she was chilled and dirty and out of sorts.

"The little monsters," she muttered.

Kaeldra felt her way back to her provisions again, lit her torch and, carrying her things in her skirt, ventured back to the edge of the inner cavern. Kneeling, she dug the end of her torch into the sand, flattened herself against a recess in the wall, then peeked inside, not wanting to be ambushed again.

Illuminated by a shaft of sunlight, a dracling strutted round the cavern, trailing Kaeldra's tattered blanket from its teeth. A smaller one, crouching, crept stealthily behind. Their birdlike talons seemed too large for their bodies; they moved with the clumsy stiffness of all young things. Yet there was an odd, lilting buoyancy to the draclings' gait, as if they were inflated with air.

The little dracling made its move. It galloped toward the blanket and took a flying leap, its talons outstretched. At the last moment, the other dracling casually twitched the blanket away. The little one yowled plaintively and plunged to the ground, its talons clutching sand.

The next instant, the big reddish dracling plummeted through the air from its hiding place atop a tall boulder. It smacked down on the first dracling's back, flattening it. The smitten dracling howled and turned to fight. Over and over they rolled, nipping and growling, the blanket forgotten.

But the littlest one remembered. It peered from side to side as if it couldn't believe its luck. Then it streaked to the blanket, snatched it in its teeth, and bolted.

Kaeldra laughed aloud.

The draclings froze. They gawked at Kaeldra; then there was a sudden mad scramble for a rocky outcrop behind them.

"It's all right," Kaeldra said softly. "I won't hurt you."

No movement.

"Don't you remember me? I was here before." Slowly, she crept forward into the cavern.

A narrow head poked up from behind a rock. The middle-sized one, Kaeldra saw, the one that had paraded the blanket. It regarded her fiercely and snorted out a small, blue smoke-puff.

Stifling a smile, Kaeldra knelt on the floor at the center of the cavern. She emptied her provisions into the sand and separated out the food: five dried seaplums, a hunk of smoked rabbit meat, a wedge of cheese, four pilfur biscuits. She sat by the food, talking softly.

One by one, the draclings' heads appeared above the rocks. They stared at Kaeldra. They stared at the food. Then at last, the middle-sized one tiptoed toward her down the rock pile, and through the light patch that pooled across the sand.

Kaeldra did not move. The dracling sniffed at the

cheese wedge. It picked it up in its talons and turned it over. It flicked at it with its long forked tongue. Still warily eyeing Kaeldra, it gulped the cheese whole.

With that the reddish dracling bounded forward and attacked the meat, the little one fast behind. Sooner than Kaeldra would have believed possible, the food was gone, and the draclings were snuffling about, hoping for more. The big one approached Kaeldra, nibbled her boot.

"Ouch!" Kaeldra cried. "That's not to eat!" She reached for her waterskin. The big dracling nipped it. "No!" Kaeldra snatched the skin away. Quickly, she unstoppered it, soaked a corner of her gown and held it over her lap. The dracling bit off a hunk of cloth. "No, no! To *drink*!" Kaeldra trickled a thread of water onto the dracling's nose. It backed away, blinking, shaking its head. Then it flicked its tongue and slowly crept near.

Kaeldra wrung the water out of her gown. The dracling flicked its tongue to catch the drops. Soon all three draclings were gathered around her lap, flicking their long forked tongues, drinking. They were larger than before, the size of foxes, only longer. Up close, Kaeldra saw that they were moulting. Their skins looked like too-tight suits of clothes, bursting at the seams, peeling away at heads and claws, exposing row upon row of tiny new scales, thin and translucent as a baby's fingernails. The big one's scales had a mottled, coppery red tint; the other two were a pale yellow-green.

Gently, Kaeldra touched the middle-sized one. She stroked the bony ridges above its eyes. She ran her hand across its pointy crest and down the serrated ridges that jutted from its spine. Fiora's crest and ridge were rigid; the draclings' were soft and floppy.

A gentle vibration began in Kaeldra's head, a sort of thrumming that she felt rather than heard. The middle-sized dracling tipped up its head and flicked its tongue at her cheek, its throat vibrating like the low string on a harp. Its breath was warm. It smelled like burnt toast. The big one gently nibbled and sucked at her fingers; the littlest curled up in her lap.

And the thrumming thrummed louder until it pulsed through her blood: the music of dragons inside her.

chapter 9

And dragons, being kin to avian beings, oft commune
with birds, and eat not the flesh thereof.
—*The Bok of Dragon*

Kaeldra went often to care for the draclings, almost
every quarter-moon. She left before dawn and took a
roundabout route so the dragon hunters could not track
her. They seemed not to be searching near Myrrathog
in any event, but somewhere to the south. Each time,
she returned with milk; Lyf improved day by day. Each
time, Fiora extracted from Kaeldra a promise to return.

The draclings greeted her at the cave mouth when
she came. They pushed their noses against her, looking
for treats. Kaeldra brought them nuts and dried apples
and cheeses. They especially liked the cheese.

Sometimes the draclings jostled her so hard she

nearly fell. "Settle down," Kaeldra would say, laughing, until once, after Fiora had left, she did fall, and there was a burning along her wrist. Blood welled in dark drops from a long, jagged scratch. "Now look what you've done," Kaeldra cried. She blotted the blood with a corner of her gown, and at once there was a jolt in her mind, a sudden sadness.

And the middle-sized dracling was looking at her, was *regarding* her as if it had said something and expected a reply.

"It's all right," Kaeldra said, although the wound still burned. "Only a cut."

The dracling tipped its narrow head and flicked its tongue at Kaeldra's cheek. It, like the others, had shed its baby skin and gleamed, head to tail, with hard, mottle-hued scales. Only their back ridges and undersides were soft; and there, on the leathery hide just below this dracling's jaw line, Kaeldra scratched. The dracling thrummed, its eyes glazing over in bliss. Such a sweet thing, Kaeldra thought. And I don't even have a name for you.

There was a tingling sensation in her head, a prickling that gathered and grew until it made a word in her mind: ⟨Embyr.⟩

"Embyr," Kaeldra said, trying it on her tongue. "Is that your name?"

Looking into the green dracling's eyes, she knew that it was.

The largest dracling nudged Kaeldra's elbow, knocking her arm away from Embyr. Kaeldra laughed. "Do you want to tell me your name, too?" She held its head in her hands, stroked the copper red scales. "All right. I'm listening."

⟨Pyro,⟩ she felt.

And Kaeldra knew, although she did not know how she knew, that Pyro was a male, whereas Embyr was female.

Something touched Kaeldra's arm. The smallest dracling licked her fingers.

⟨Synge.⟩

"Oh, Synge," Kaeldra said, and gathered the little green female into her lap. Synge nibbled at Kaeldra's fingers. Life pulsed in the dracling's throat.

There was a sudden clattering, and Kaeldra looked round to see her blanket roll unrolled, its contents strewn across the sand. Embyr and Pyro nosed about, looking for something to eat.

"Get away from there! Stop that!" Kaeldra reached into her pocket and tossed them a handful of whisple nuts.

The draclings lunged, captured the nuts in their claws and crunched them with their thin, sharp teeth.

Kaeldra sighed as she gathered up her things.

Hungry. Always hungry.

Pyro poked her with his nose, nipped at her skirt. Kaeldra jumped up and yanked her skirt away. "Stop it, Pyro! You've had enough."

The dracling cocked a mournful eye at her. ⟨Hungry.⟩

"Your mother fed you before she left."

⟨Hungry.⟩

"No. I can't feed you anymore now. We won't have anything for later." A wave of emotion hit her, an aching and a sadness and a hunger. "Oh, very well." Kaeldra reached for her blanket roll, then felt a ticklishness at the edge of her mind.

Laughter?

Yes!

Pyro was laughing at her.

"You little whelp!" Kaeldra shook her fist; Pyro spun around and scampered into the passage.

They were so full of energy! All day long they darted through the cave, vaulted from boulder to boulder, pounced, wrestled, rolled. If Kaeldra refused to join in their play, they lay in ambush and tumbled her to the ground. Once, remembering the dragonslayer's story about the silver tone pipes, Kaeldra tried whistling a single high note to calm them. The draclings stilled, sleepy-eyed, until she ran out of breath, then they bounded past her in a burst of exuberance.

Kaeldra set out snares to catch small animals whenever she came. She wondered what Fiora fed the draclings. They were still nursing, but Kaeldra knew they must be eating more than just milk. She suspected that Fiora brought her kills home and hid them somewhere inside the cave, but Kaeldra never looked; she feared what she might find.

Lambs, of late, had been disappearing from the graze. Some full-grown sheep, as well. No one knew for certain what predator was responsible. Some said wolves;

71

others, a dragon. The men had vowed to track it down.

Kaeldra hoped it was wolves.

Early one morning, when Fiora had been gone for more than a day and still had not returned, Kaeldra set off for the spring to check on her snares. The draclings lounged in the sun just outside the cave, occasionally pouncing at whistle pigs. The fearless little rodents popped up from their burrow holes, whistled, and just when the draclings were upon them, disappeared into the earth again.

"If only those bunglers could catch something, I wouldn't have to do this," Kaeldra muttered.

A breeze stung her face, but the sun shone and tiny green shoots thrust up between vanishing pockets of snow.

The spring bubbled up from the ground, forming a shallow pool in the rocks. Kaeldra went from snare to snare, but her take was not good; of seven snares, she netted only a whistle pig and a rabbit. The last snare held a whimble thrush, which saddened Kaeldra. The draclings mourned when she brought dead birds, refusing to eat them, although they felt no compunction about devouring anything else.

Kaeldra closed her game sack and tied it with a leather thong. If only they didn't eat so *much*. Hoisting the sack over her shoulder, she started back up to the cave.

A sudden pain shot through her head. She heard a high-pitched cry from somewhere up the mountain, and a chattering of birds.

The draclings.

Kaeldra ran, slipping on loose scree, scraping her knees. A flurry of whitchils circled and dove up ahead. When at last the cave came into view, she gasped and dropped her bag.

It was a wolf.

It lunged for Synge's neck. The dracling twisted; the wolf missed her neck but buried its teeth in her back ridge. Synge flailed and cried and beat her flimsy wings. She was as large as the wolf, but it was stronger; it was dragging her away. Synge lashed at it with her tail. The wolf yipped, let go and backed off, waiting for a chance to pounce.

"Get out of here!" Kaeldra ran toward the wolf, waving her arms. She picked up a sharp rock and hurled it at it; the wolf dodged and crept closer to Synge.

A second wolf prowled by the cave mouth. Pyro cowered just inside. Embyr, ever the bold one, charged the wolf, snorted smoke, then scrambled back into the cave.

"Go away!" Kaeldra pitched another rock; it nicked the first wolf's ear. She threw again and heard a solid whack. The wolf yelped, pawing at its snout. "Go!" Kaeldra advanced upon the wolf, pelting it with rocks. With a last, hungry glance at Synge, it fled with its companion, pursued by a whirl of birds.

Kaeldra chased the wolves, peppering them with rocks, until their hunched forms disappeared behind a stony hummock. Then she spun round and dashed back to Synge, who lay gasping and whimpering just outside the cave.

Gently, Kaeldra fingered all around Synge's throat

and neck and back. No break in the hard, light green scales near her spine. No break in the skin at her throat. Kaeldra felt Synge all over: her back, her belly, her tail. She coaxed open the dracling's wings, gossamer as spider spin.

Except for a serrated nick in her back ridge, Synge was not hurt. Kaeldra gathered her up and carried her back into the second cavern, wondering again at how light she was.

She laid Synge in the puddle of sunshine from the hole in the roof, then turned to Embyr and Pyro, who had followed. "Now, stay! Both of you! Don't move until I get back!"

Kaeldra sprinted outside and returned with the game sack. She set the whistle pig on the sand in front of Synge, who suddenly stopped whimpering and fell upon the kill. Pyro inched toward the whistle pig, snuffling. "Oh, no you don't. That's for Synge. You and Embyr share this." Kaeldra tossed them the rabbit.

The draclings ripped open their kill, demolished the bloody meat. Kaeldra turned her head. She was glad to see that Synge had not lost her appetite, but she couldn't bear to watch the draclings eat. They're like wild animals, she thought; and then, surprised that she had forgotten, they *are* wild animals.

Embyr and Pyro, having made short work of their rabbit, began to slink toward Synge.

"No!" Kaeldra said again. "That is Synge's."

⟨Hungry,⟩ Pyro protested.

"Well, you'll just have to wait until your mother

gets home," Kaeldra said, irritated at Fiora for staying away so long.

Pyro scampered down the passage.

"Pyro! You come back. Pyro!" Kaeldra ran into the passage and listened in the dark. He wouldn't be foolish enough to go outside the cave again, would he?

There. A rustling. He was coming back. Pyro materialized in the darkness—Pyro and something else, something he was dragging. It looked vaguely like a blanket, only heavier, perhaps. But it wasn't her blanket. That was behind her in the cavern. Where would he get another blanket?

Pyro drew closer, dragging the thing. He dropped it and ran to Kaeldra.

⟨Hungry,⟩ he said.

Kaeldra stared.

It wasn't a blanket. It was a lamb. The bloody, eaten carcass of a lamb.

chapter 10

May your groom in his sleep snore not.
                    —Elythian wedding toast

"Look, Kael!" Lyf's little fingers tightened around Kael-dra's own. "Someone's coming!"

Clouds fled across the sky as if chased by a pack of wolves. A long shadow wound down across the hillside from the west, a horse and rider at its tail.

"It's likely Jeorg Sigrad," Kaeldra said. The Kragish youth had visited often since that first night, but stayed only when Granmyr was gone. He told tales of ancient dragons while Ryfenn and Mirym plied him with honey cakes and brew. He did not again ask Kaeldra about dragons; nor did he mention the green in her eyes.

Still, Kaeldra felt her shoulders stiffen. Ever since

76

the day the Elythian men had come seeking her, dreams of horsemen had filled her nights. She would wake suddenly and sit up in the dark, palms damp, blood pounding in her throat like hoofbeats.

"Master Jeorg! Master Jeorg! I hope it's Master Jeorg!" Lyf did a little dance. Dark hairwisps escaped her woolen headwrap and whipped across her face. Lyf grabbed Kaeldra's hands, spun her around. Kaeldra, looking down at her, felt light inside. Lyf was well again. That's what Granmyr had said. Well enough to come watch the flock with Kaeldra as before.

The horseman grew larger. His shadow rippled across a moving sea of gorse and bracken. It *was* Jeorg, she saw. He would be disappointed that it was she, and not Mirym, who watched the sheep today.

Jeorg reined in his horse and jumped to the ground. "Kaeldra!" he said. "You've returned!" He turned to Lyf, lifted her high over his head. His cloak billowed and snapped in the wind.

"Let me down! Let me down!" Lyf shrieked, delighted.

He laughed. "And how's my Lyfling?" he said.

His Lyfling? That was *Kaeldra's* special name for Lyf. It didn't sound right when he said it.

"Mirym's at the cottage," Kaeldra said.

Jeorg set down Lyf. He tousled her hair, then pulled her headwrap snug over her head. "I wasn't looking for Mirym." He straightened. "I came to talk to you."

Kaeldra felt the warmth rush to her face. "What about?"

"Ah," the young man hesitated, as if uncertain how to begin. "Sheep," he said at last.

"Oh." Kaeldra turned away, surprised by a twinge of disappointment. A jackdaw called hoarsely, tilted in a sudden air gust.

". . . eight sheep missing," he was saying. "Calyffs have lost ten. Nearly every farm in the district has lost three or four, at least. You've lost—how many?"

"Seven," Kaeldra lied. Two days ago another sheep had disappeared, making eleven all together.

"Mirym said nine some days ago."

Kaeldra shrugged.

"And the cows. Five gone. Disappeared with neither track nor bone to go by."

"Wolves," Kaeldra said. "There are many this year." Near her foot, a clump of gorse rattled in the breeze. Its blossoms looked butter soft against the prickly stalks.

"Kaeldra—"

"What can *I* do? Why are you telling *me* about this? I don't know any more than you!"

"Look," Jeorg said. "I need—" He stopped, and in his eyes she saw an unguarded plea for help. Vexed, he brushed back a lock of hair. "If you don't care about the sheep, at least you owe it to your countrymen to help. They neglect their fields to hunt the thing, but they know not the craft. Someone will die before they're through, unless you—"

"So talk to *them!* I can't do anything about it."

Lyf scampered up the hillside after a lamb. It bleated and ran to be near its mother.

Jeorg sighed, shook his head, and turned to watch

Lyf. "She's much better, now, isn't she?" he said. "The first time I saw her, she was a very sick lass. Now—look at her. As healthy a lamblet as ever I saw."

"She's not entirely well yet. We have to be careful. She gets better and worse."

"Yes, but she's almost well. Thanks be to the gods—and to that—medicine—you bring her."

A tightness coiled around Kaeldra's chest and neck. *He knows,* she thought.

"Kaeldra." He touched her shoulder. She pulled away. "I wouldn't kill it before Lyf was completely well. Tell me where it lairs, and I'll protect it from the hunters until then."

The air felt dense, hard to breathe. "I don't know what you're talking about!" *He knows.*

"Don't you? What about her eyes?" Kaeldra stared at him, uncomprehending. "Look at her eyes!" Jeorg turned and strode away, calling for Lyf. She ran to him, grabbed his hand, and tugged him down the hill. If Kaeldra had not been so frightened, she would have laughed.

"What is it?" Lyf asked. "What do you want me to show Kaeldra?" She turned from him, tilted her head up at Kaeldra. "What does he want you to see?"

Kaeldra felt a crumbling inside her, like a stone wall shaken apart in a quaking of the earth.

They were green. Lyf's eyes were flecked with green. And even more: two circles of green, the color of fir trees in the shadows, pooled around her pupils. How could she not have seen?

"Your eyes," Kaeldra whispered.

"Kael?" Lyf said. She sounded afraid. "Kael, what's wrong with my eyes?"

Kaeldra drew Lyf to her, hugged her tight. "Nothing is wrong with your eyes," she said. "They are beautiful eyes."

"Very beautiful," Jeorg agreed. "Even more beautiful than when they were brown. The green in them—" He broke off, and as his own eyes moved to gaze into Kaeldra's, she saw again the silent plea, felt the tug of an insistent current, drawing her toward him.

"Kaeldra, please," he said.

He is a dragonslayer, she told herself fiercely. He is my enemy.

"If you're worried about Lyfling—"

"I don't know what you're talking about," Kaeldra said. "Go away. Leave me alone."

Jeorg's eyes hardened. "Very well, I will." He mounted his horse and wheeled to face Kaeldra. "I warned you, Kaeldra. Remember that."

He spun his horse around and galloped away.

The horsemen were chasing her. It was night, and they were chasing her up the mountain. She was running, running to the cave, but it was far away. They were shooting arrows at her, fire-arrows, arrows that flamed through the air. There was a brightness on her eyes, there was a rushing in her ears when the fire-arrows passed.

Bright-rush.

Bright-rush.

Bright-rush.

Kaeldra opened her eyes. It was dark. She was in the cave, safe, with the draclings.

She took a deep breath to calm her bloodbeat. She smelled the smoky cave-smell, now almost as familiar as home. Safe.

Bright-rush.

Kaeldra sat up. *What was that?* She scanned the darkness. Where were the draclings?

Molten panic dripped into her chest.

Bright-rush.

Flame shot through the air! Kaeldra blinked, blinded by the sudden light burst. Something dark floated up, beyond the yellow spots that swam before her eyes. She blinked again, strained to see what floated in the dark.

It was a dracling.

It was three draclings; they drifted in the air like leaves on a still mountain lake.

Bright-rush.

One of the draclings breathed out flame. It dropped down and rose again slowly when the flaming ended.

⟨Embyr?⟩ Kaeldra reached out with her mind. Stillness. They're asleep, she realized. They were floating in their sleep, as the dragonslayer had said.

For a long time, Kaeldra watched. She saw the draclings rise through the air, saw them flame and drop and rise again. After a time, they did not rise as high, and when they dropped, they touched the ground. Soon the rising was a sigh, and the flames were only sparks. At last the draclings came to rest; only their sides rose and fell in sleep breathing.

But Kaeldra slept no more that night. She lay awake and thought—of horsemen, of green eyes, of dragons that flame and fly—until the cave walls glowed pink with dawn.

chapter 11

For let a man knead pitch and fat and straw into gobs;
and with these let him tempte the fire-drake: so will
the foule beast eat and burst to smithers.

—*Dragonslayer's Guyde*

Ungry.⟩

Kaeldra roused. Three pairs of slotted green eyes
were cocked at her. Pyro pushed at her cheek with his
nose.

⟨Hungry.⟩

Kaeldra yawned and stretched. Yellow light streamed
in through the gap in the roof. She had lain down sometime after sunrise; now it must be midmorning, at least.

⟨Hungry. Hungry. Hungry.⟩ Encouraged, the draclings nudged at her face and neck. Their complaints
pelted her mind like a hail of pebbles, made it impossible
to think.

"Stop it!" Kaeldra said, laughing. She curled herself into a protective ball. The draclings prodded her, tickled her. Thrumming, they clambered onto her back. "Oh, all right," Kaeldra groaned. She stood; the draclings slid down and landed in a heap. She stumbled through the cave; the draclings pounced at her feet. Her head felt heavy and dull. Not enough sleep. At the cave mouth she turned. "I'm going for food. You stay!"

She took two paces, then spun around to check. Pyro, halfway out of the cave, quickly slunk back in.

"Stay! I mean it, Pyro." She hoped she sounded firm enough. If they got out and started floating, she didn't know what she would do.

At the spring, Kaeldra drank deeply, then splashed water on her face. A smudge of rainbow blurred across the droplets on her lashes. There was a quick flash of light; the droplets burned her eyes like tiny suns.

Startled, Kaeldra dashed the water from her eyes. And then the pain came. It grew until her cheeks and temples pulsed with it. It grew until her whole head swelled with it, drummed with it, seemed to split and burst with it.

Kaeldra cried out and dug her palms into her face.

The pain pulsed once, pulsed twice, pulsed three times more. And then began to shrink. Slowly, it shrank until it wasn't pain anymore, but only an echo: a lingering ringing-in-the-ears of pain.

Kaeldra opened her eyes. The springwater splashed against the rocks. There was a trembling in the air, a low rumble that crashed and echoed like distant thunder.

What is it?

Dizzy, Kaeldra staggered back toward the cave. Something still hurt inside her head, but not like the pain before. This hurt was small and sharp, like crying.

It *was* crying. The draclings were crying.

Kaeldra ran. She scrambled across the loose rocks, stooping to grab a handful. The wolves. Must stop the wolves.

But there were no wolves. Only draclings. Outside the cave. They staggered about, jostled one another, bumped into boulders. The crying was loud in Kaeldra's mind.

No wolves.

"What is it?" Kaeldra asked, but the draclings paid no heed. The crying was so loud now that Kaeldra couldn't tell whether she were really hearing it or just feeling it inside her head. She ran to Embyr, picked her up, set her down inside the cave. Then she pushed Synge in, but Embyr was already stumbling out. "Stay!" Kaeldra cried, but the draclings seemed not to know her or what they were doing. She shoved Embyr in again and ran to get Pyro. She threw him in; Embyr and Synge were out. Kaeldra stood at the cave mouth blocking one dracling, grabbing for the others, trying to keep them inside.

What is it?

Pyro pounced and streaked past her out of the cave. She wheeled around, snatched at him, missed.

"Come back here!" she cried. And then stood still, staring out across the valley.

Away in the south, a smoke plume curled lazily in

the kollflower-blue sky. A ring of gnatlike specks swam round the smoke. But they weren't gnats, Kaeldra knew. They were birds, all kinds of birds, more birds than Kaeldra had ever seen together at once. Through the crying, she could hear their calls.

Kaeldra suddenly felt as if she had swallowed a stone. Something awful had happened, she knew that. But what?

She turned to Embyr. ⟨What is it?⟩ she demanded. She cupped the dracling's head in her hands. ⟨Talk to me! Tell me what it is!⟩

Embyr's eyes met Kaeldra's. Her crying stopped. Then it began again, only this time, Kaeldra understood. She threw her arms around the dracling's neck as the wail ripped through her head:

⟨Motherrr!⟩

chapter 12

Into the sky
The dragon doth fly
A terror of flame, fang, and coil.

Yet soon all below
The dragonpods grow
And fruitful becomes the burnt soil.

—Anonymous,
From the archives of Rog

〈Hush. Wait here.〉

The draclings' narrow heads turned to follow as Kaeldra crept away from them. Embyr leaned forward, rose to her feet in a single, fluid movement.

〈No, Embyr. Lie still. I'll soon return.〉

In the darkness, the draclings looked like three boulders in a stand of rock near the clayhouse. But then the bright half-moon slipped out from behind a cloud, and the dragon backs gleamed like hammered brass.

No one would be out this time of night, Kaeldra told herself. No one would see. At least, not on an ordinary night.

But nothing seemed ordinary anymore.

Kaeldra felt her way over the familiar ground to the clayhouse. The door was partway open. Firelight licked at the darkness inside. Not ordinary. Why would Granmyr be up now, in the stillness before dawn? Was she waiting for her? Did she know of Fiora's death? Kaeldra thought of Jeorg, of the hunters who had come seeking her. Maybe it wasn't Granmyr at all, but someone else, someone tricking her, someone who knew where she would go.

Kaeldra hesitated. For the thousandth time she asked herself if she had done the right thing, bringing the draclings here. But Fiora was dead. Of that, Kaeldra was certain. And the draclings couldn't take care of themselves. She couldn't trust them to stay in the cave when she was away. And then there were the wolves— and whoever had killed Fiora.

Something thumped inside the clayhouse.

Fear flicked up the back of Kaeldra's neck.

Another thump and then another. A steady, rhythmic hum: the sound of Granmyr at her wheel.

Kaeldra drew in a breath, peered through the doorway.

Granmyr looked up.

"Child," Granmyr said, and then she was holding Kaeldra in her arms. *Safe.* Kaeldra felt again how thin Granmyr was, how light. But even so, she felt safe, completely safe, for the first time since Fiora had died nearly a day ago.

Granmyr drew back. "Did you bring them with you?"

Kaeldra nodded. She did not ask how Granmyr guessed she had the draclings. "Outside," Kaeldra said.

"Quickly. Bring them in."

Kaeldra stepped out, called silently for her charges. Slowly, three heads appeared from behind the rocks. The draclings slunk toward the doorway and rubbed against Kaeldra's legs, but did not go in.

"Quickly," Granmyr said. "Jeorg Sigrad was here earlier with his falcon. He inquired for you. We may be watched."

"Did he do it? Did he kill Fiora?"

"No. It was that gang of local fools. They baited her with a concoction of pitch and straw. She ate it and exploded, killing two of them. This, for the glory of Elythia, mind you. Then they put the dragon's head on a cart and paraded it through the town. Idiots!"

Kaeldra's stomach lurched. We're safe now, she told herself. We're with Granmyr. Granmyr will take care of us.

The draclings stared at the old woman. A fearing and a puzzlement tickled at Kaeldra's mind.

⟨It's all right.⟩ Untangling her feet from the little ones, Kaeldra walked into the clayhouse. She laid her hand on Granmyr's shoulder. ⟨Safe.⟩

Embyr crept into the room, rubbed against Kaeldra's legs. Kaeldra bent and stroked her head. Then Pyro and Synge inched forward, side by side, ready to bolt. Embyr sniffed at Granmyr's feet. A soft thrumming began in her throat. One by one, the three draclings began to mill about Granmyr's legs, rubbing, thrumming. Firelight played on their backs, glittered coppery red and green.

Granmyr knelt, reached to touch them. She cradled their heads in her hands, looked into their eyes. Synge nuzzled her stomach; the old woman sat back and gathered the baby dragon into her lap. The thrumming built to a gentle roar.

Granmyr looked up. "I never thought—" her voice broke. Her eyes were glistening, Kaeldra saw with surprise. "I never thought to see *this*," Granmyr whispered.

Softly, Kaeldra shut the door.

After a time the draclings ventured from Granmyr and began to explore. They sniffed at the wet clay, drank from the waterpot. They tiptoed around the stacks of bisque, played hide and seek in large urns. ⟨Careful,⟩ Kaeldra warned, but they walked lightly and disturbed nothing.

Praise the heavens they were over their craziness. They were themselves again, only more subdued. Except they had not spoken. They had said nothing since last morning, when it had happened.

Granmyr passed Kaeldra a mug of tea and gestured for her to sit on a stool near the fire. "What will we do now, Granmyr?" Kaeldra asked, feeling the tea warm inside her, feeling the fire heat touch her face and hands and knees.

Granmyr stirred the fire with a long stick. Yellow light burst across her face. Kaeldra waited.

"What do you think?" Granmyr asked.

Kaeldra had thought about it. She had thought about it all the way down the mountain. Someone had to care for the draclings. Someone who understood them;

someone whom they could trust. But Kaeldra didn't see how they could stay here, on the croft. Sooner or later, the wrong people would find them: Jeorg or the men of Elythia.

And another thing: What would the draclings eat? They couldn't survive on small animals forever. They were growing fast. Soon they would need larger prey. Few hart roamed these hills, and fewer wypari. But one kind of meat was plentiful, and the draclings already had a taste for it. All too soon, Kaeldra knew, the draclings would hunt for sheep.

Kaeldra had thought about it, but she didn't like what she had thought. She wanted Granmyr to think. She wanted Granmyr to make it right.

"Couldn't they stay here?" Kaeldra asked. "You could make a spell to protect them. You could . . ."

Kaeldra remembered what Granmyr had said before when she had asked the old woman to make Lyf well with her magic. Her magic was weak, she had said. The safe feeling that had welled up inside her shrank to a small, hard lump in her stomach.

"I couldn't go away from here," Kaeldra said. Granmyr had said nothing about her going away, but she felt she needed to say it. "Lyf needs me. How will she get well without the . . ." Kaeldra stopped. There was no more milk, she remembered. Fiora was dead.

"Lyf is better now. She will be fine."

"But her eyes . . ."

Granmyr stirred the fire again. "There's nothing wrong with Lyf's eyes," she said. "They are simply unusual. She may turn out to be a very unusual—a very singular girl. Like you."

"I don't want to be singular! I just want to stay here and *belong,* like everybody else."

There was a crash behind her. The draclings scrambled away and disappeared behind a stacked pile of bowls. Shards from a large bisque crock littered the ground. Kaeldra sighed and went to pick up the pieces. "I'm sorry. I should have been watching. I should have—"

"It's not your fault, child."

"Anyway, where would I take them? I have no place to go."

"There is a place," Granmyr said.

Kaeldra sighed again. There *would* be. She felt her familiar world begin to slip away from her. Why couldn't everything have stayed the way it was? She would have tried even harder to look and act as an Elythian girl ought. She would have *made* Ryfenn like her; she would have *made* herself belong, in time.

"Come," Granmyr said. She took the shards out of Kaeldra's hands and led her to a straw pallet in a corner of the shed. "You need your rest. I will arrange what needs to be arranged."

"Why can't I sleep in the loft? I want to sleep in the loft."

Granmyr pulled a blanket over her. "It is best you not see the others before you go. If they know nothing, they can give nothing away."

"But I have to say good-bye to Ryfenn and Lyf and Mirym! I can't go without seeing them. I can't—"

Kaeldra tried to sit up, but an immense tiredness weighed her down. As though looking up from the bottom of a well, Kaeldra watched Granmyr turn in the light, watched her sit at her wheel. The wheel sounds echoed faintly, as if through water.

She awoke to the smells of soup and hot bread. Pewter gray, the light of dusk trickled through the clay-house window. She must have slept all day! Granmyr was feeding the draclings. She broke off chunks of cheese, and they lifted them from her open palm with their tongues.

The old woman looked up from the draclings and smiled. There was a softness to her face that Kaeldra seldom saw there. "You're awake," she said.

She brought Kaeldra soup, bread, and a wedge of cheese. The soup was thick and good. Something nagged at the back of Kaeldra's mind, something unpleasant. She shrugged and pushed it away.

Pyro sniffed at Granmyr's sleeve, searching for more cheese. He looked at Kaeldra. ⟨Hungry.⟩

⟨You're always hungry,⟩ Kaeldra thought, then realized: He spoke! For the first time since—

⟨Hungry.⟩

Kaeldra felt the reproach in his voice. *She* was eating, but she'd forgotten about feeding them. The draclings hadn't had any meat since they had left the cave. She ought to have set snares that morning.

"Have you fed them aught but cheese?" Kaeldra asked.

Granmyr looked at Kaeldra, then at Pyro, then back

93

at Kaeldra. "He said something to you, didn't he?" she said. "And you answered."

"He said he's hungry. They eat a lot."

"I tried to talk to them," Granmyr mused. "But I felt no reply. How do you know when they're—talking to you?"

"You feel it in your head. Sometimes it's words, and sometimes it's just a feeling. It tingles, with the little ones, although when Fiora talked, it pained me." Fiora. Kaeldra put down her soup. "I felt her die."

Granmyr touched Kaeldra's hand. Kaeldra tried to blink back the tears, but they came anyway, and then Granmyr was holding her. All the bad things she had tried to forget came flooding back. Fiora dead. No one else to care for the draclings. Having to go away, go somewhere strange, somewhere she'd never been. Having to leave without saying good-bye to Lyf or Mirym or Ryfenn. Kaeldra's nose was running; Granmyr's rough gown scratched her cheek, but Kaeldra didn't care. The dragonslayer—

"I don't want to go," Kaeldra whispered, and remembered, as she spoke them, having said those words before. It seemed that Granmyr was always sending her on journeys she did not want to take.

The draclings gathered round, nuzzling her. Granmyr stroked her hair. "I know it's hard, child. But you're stronger than you know, and I can help a little."

Kaeldra wiped her eyes and nose on her sleeve. "Better feed the draclings," she said. "Do you have any meat?"

"Only a rabbit I caught for supper. I fed them more cheese earlier, and most of the soup. The big one tipped it over and I just managed to salvage enough for you."

"They need more, I think." Kaeldra wondered how she would feed them from now on.

"I'll see what I can find," Granmyr said. Soon she returned with the rabbit, more cheese, some dried meat, and a few eggs. The draclings tore into them, ravenous, as Kaeldra finished her meal. When the draclings had done, they curled up near the fire and slept.

"Here. Put on these." Granmyr set a pile of woven stuff on her lap.

Kaeldra touched the cloth. It was drab and coarsely woven, not like her own things, the soft, pastel-hued garments that she herself had carefully woven and dyed. She sorted out shift and stockings, underhood and gown. The gown seemed wrong, somehow. It seemed too short. And the shift—Kaeldra held up the oddly shaped garment. It wasn't a shift. It was—breeches!

"These are *boys'* things!"

"A girl is not safe on the road. Neither is a boy, for that matter, but for a girl it is worse." Speculatively, Granmyr fingered Kaeldra's long braid. "Now, this—"

"No!" Kaeldra cried. She snatched away her braid. "Then people would think I was a boy."

"Well, that's the idea, isn't it?" Granmyr said dryly, but for the moment she said no more about the braid.

Kaeldra put on the garments. The tunic felt strange and short. The breeches bunched between her legs. Her own gown, fashioned in the way of Elythia, lay upon the floor. A lump rose in her throat. Stripped of her familiar garb, she felt as conspicuous as a heron in a flock of doves.

"Don't forget the hood," Granmyr said. "You'll have to wear it night and day—unless we cut your hair."

Kaeldra quickly yanked the hood over her head.

Granmyr slipped a rope around Kaeldra's waist and tied on a leather purse, heavy with coins. She nodded at the bulging blanket roll on the table. "I packed rope and an extra blanket so you can tie them down at night. They float in their sleep."

"I know," Kaeldra said.

Granmyr looked at Kaeldra. She shook her head as though in wonderment, leading Kaeldra to the wheel. "All these years I've asked myself whether you inherited the gift. Even so, I underestimated you."

"But where will I go? You said there is a place."

"Watch."

Granmyr wet her hands, laid them on the red clay. It spun, rose, shimmered like distant hills in the summer heat. Between Granmyr's fingers, the clay began to glow. The glow spread, spread until the whole clay lump shone white. White walls rose up out of it, white turrets, white spires. A tiny white banner trembled, unfurled, buffeted by a spectral breeze.

"There," Granmyr murmured. "Just as I thought."

Her hands rose to touch the banner. It swelled and darkened until Kaeldra saw that it was a bird, a bird cupped in Granmyr's hands. The bird cocked its head, gave a sudden cry. A kestrel's cry. There was a blur of feathers, a beating of wings. A dark shape streaked through the window into the dark.

Kaeldra heard Granmyr's sharp intake of breath. "A changing," the old woman said. "I have outdone myself this night."

The clay slowed, the glow dimmed, the castle caved in upon itself.

Granmyr dipped her hands into the waterpot to wash off the slip and, drying them, turned to Kaeldra. "That castle is where you must go. It is the fastness of the Sentinels, on the island of Rog, off the northern coast of Kragrom. Seek there the man called Landerath. He will help."

"But you said the Sentinels are dragonslayers! And Landerath—is he not the one who sent Jeorg?"

"He is. You will have need of much caution. Yet Landerath is not what he seems. Though he leads the Sentinels, in truth he is friend—not foe—to dragons. He, too, witnessed the Migration. Smitten with awe he was, and filled with purpose. He pledged secret loyalty to Kara; they and a handful of others plotted to save the hatchlings when the next hatching cycle commenced.

"They formed an underground of informants, spanning the four corners of the earth. Each informant was given a seabird, color banded and trained to return at first to Kara, and then, after her death, to Landerath. From time to time old birds were replaced with young ones. At the first sign of a hatching the informant was to release the bird—"

"The seabird! You released it and—"

"Landerath knew by the color of the band from whence it came."

"Then why did he send Jeorg? He is a slayer, not a friend."

Granmyr shook her head. "That young man is lying about something, but I cannot divine his purpose. Landerath was to have sent a dragon friend to protect the hatchlings—not a slayer. And yet if Jeorg knew this, why would he not at least pretend to be a friend? And how came he to possess Landerath's brooch, which he showed me when he first arrived? It is the very brooch, wrought in the shape of a dragonpod bloom, that I gave Landerath long ago in Kragrom. As a token of—esteem, I think I said. What bletherchaff!" Granmyr smiled wryly. "I was moondaft in love with him, but he had a calling, and—" She shook her head again, breaking out of her reverie, then stood and began to tie the blanket roll across Kaeldra's back.

"What is this dragonpod bloom?" Kaeldra asked. "You spoke of it once before, and I know it not."

"You have never seen one; they disappeared not long after the Migration. They had ice blue petals and brought untold fertility to the soil. The flowers grew, the old ones said, after a flight of dragons.

"But of Jeorg, I like it not. Were he a dragon friend, he would have told me by now. I am uneasy for Landerath." Granmyr cinched the last knot and tugged at the rope to test it. "In any case, you must not let Jeorg find you."

"But this Landerath," Kaeldra stalled. "When I reach him, then what? What will he do?"

"I know not for certain. He may know where the dragonkyn dwells and have means of sending the draclings there. Or at the very least—" Granmyr hesitated. "He knows the name of the dragon leader. He knows the location of the council bluff, where Kara summoned the dragons and where they promised to return. Landerath is not a dragon-sayer; he may not call. But you—" Abruptly, Granmyr picked up a sheepskin cloak and placed it over Kaeldra's shoulders. "I doubt it will come to that. Time it is for you to go."

She led Kaeldra to the doorway. The dragons, awake now, prowled at her feet. She could feel their restlessness as if it were a live thing inside her. Yet Kaeldra, filled with dread, hung back, her mind groping for some reason not to go.

"But how will I find it?" she asked. "I'll never find that fortress."

"The bird," Granmyr said.

"The bird?"

"Hush. Listen."

Silence. Then, far away, a thin, shrill cry. A kestrel's cry.

"Follow it," Granmyr said. She hugged Kaeldra again, then abruptly let go. Her eyes, for the second time that day, glistened.

"Now go."

chapter 13

Yet herein lies the peril: as the falcon finds the
dragon, the dragon feels the finding.

—*Dragonslayer's Guyde*

Not until dawn did Kaeldra know that they were
followed.

The kestrel had led them north of Myrrathog. They
must turn east, she knew: over the mountains to the sea,
over the sea to Kragrom, then over the sea again, to the
island of Rog. But soon Kaeldra had lost all sense of
direction. The moonlit landscape flowed around them:
a confusion of winding sheep paths, of crowded forests,
of wind and rock and stunted trees.

Often the kestrel disappeared, and Kaeldra was left
to stumble on with no guide. But just as fear would begin
to swell in her throat, she would hear the cry, feel the
wingbeat, see the dark flying form ahead.

"Kiree! Kiree!"

Now the kestrel swooped past, soared over the next rise. Cresting the hill, Kaeldra looked down into a soft darkness of trees. There was a rushing of water, a freshness of air.

A stream.

The draclings tumbled lightly down the slope. They pranced and drank in the stream, sent up a silvery spray.

Kaeldra followed. She plunged her hands into the water and drank until her throat ached with cold.

The moon drifted through the trees. The air was sweet with fir. From nearby came a ring owl's muted whoot.

Kaeldra shivered. She felt a sudden unease, as if something had shadowed the moon. The draclings stood still, eyes to the sky.

⟨What is it?⟩ she asked.

She reached for an answer, and the earth dipped under her feet, stars wheeling and swaying around her.

Kaeldra touched her temples. I'm hungry, she thought. That's all. She clambered up an outcropping of boulders and opened her blanket roll. The draclings surged up the rocks, shaking off water in luminous sheets. She gave each a hunk of dried meat, then tore off some for herself. Only hunger. She stretched out her legs, flexed her feet.

⟨Hungry.⟩ Pyro nosed at the blanket.

As always. Kaeldra tore off more meat for the draclings. There had better be hart where they were going. Or bear or wypari or something else big. Well, Kaeldra thought, that was not her concern. She would deliver the draclings to this Landerath, and he would get them to their kyn.

She wondered, not for the first time, how Jeorg had come to possess Landerath's brooch. Was he a thief as well as a slayer? He did not seem so.

Kaeldra shivered again. Jeorg. When she set out, she had listened for the hoofbeats, for the gyrfalcon's cry. But even the dragonslayer could not have tracked them in the dark, she told herself. Not this far.

Abruptly, she wrapped the remaining food, rolled it up in the blanket. ⟨That is enough. We must save some for later.⟩

⟨More,⟩ Pyro demanded. ⟨Hungry.⟩

⟨Hungry. Hungry,⟩ Embyr and Synge chimed in.

⟨No. No more. You can have more later.⟩ The draclings pressed around her, sniffed at the blanket roll. Pyro bit it, clamped on with his teeth. ⟨No, Pyro! Let go! Give it to me!⟩ Pyro tugged. Kaeldra yanked back. There was a ripping sound; a flap of blanket hung ragged from the roll.

May they burst from eating so much! The thought came to Kaeldra before she could squelch it. They needed more meat every day. A mountain of meat! She saw herself suddenly, standing next to Myrrathog. Only the mountain wasn't made of rock. It was made of meat. Raw meat. She was scooping out handfuls and flinging them at three grown dragons.

Where would she ever get that much meat?

Pyro nudged her hand; Kaeldra jerked it away. ⟨Oh, stop it!⟩ She would never find enough meat, never. She stared at the stream.

But of course!

She rummaged through the blanket roll. There. A candle. She held it in front of Pyro.

⟨Flame!⟩ she thought.

Puzzlement.

Kaeldra closed her eyes. She pictured in her mind a flame, flickering above the candle.

⟨Flame!⟩ The candlelight danced in her mind. ⟨Flame!⟩

Bright-rush! Hot air scorched her cheek.

The candle slumped pathetically, but it was lit. Blue smoke wisps trailed from Embyr's nostrils.

Kaeldra laughed. ⟨Good girl!⟩ She stroked Embyr's head; the dracling thrummed. Then she knelt by the stream, held the candle low over the water as she had learned when she stayed out with the flock all night in the high country. Something flashed. Kaeldra grabbed for it. Missed! Another flash. This time when she reached, something cool and slippery lurched in her hand. She tossed the fish onto the bank. Pyro pounced; in a gulp it was gone.

Flash again! Kaeldra reached, but Embyr was quicker. With a single swipe of her talons, she flipped the fish out of the water onto the bank.

The draclings learned fast. Kaeldra merely held the candle; before long the stream bank glistened with fish and spray and happy draclings. They ate until their sides bulged, until dawn bled up through the trees to the sky.

"Kreekreekreekreekree!"

The kestrel burst through the trees, streaked across the stream, calling wildly.

"Wha—?" Kaeldra stared after it, into the woods. Then from far away came the sound she had dreaded, a sound that pricked at the flesh on her back.

A gyrfalcon's cry.

The dragonslayer. She knew it was his bird as surely as if she had seen him release it. He was following them, and he was near.

The cry came again, fainter, farther.

⟨Hurry! Let's go.⟩ Kaeldra blew out the candle, tied up the torn blanket roll. They crossed the stream and plunged into the wood.

When all of the stars had faded, the kestrel led them to a cave. It was a small cave, much smaller than the dragon den. Kaeldra dared not make a fire. Quickly, she set snares in a stand of scrubby firs a little way below. She dragged a heap of brush to the cave, stacked it in front of the opening from inside, then curled up among the draclings and slipped into a restless sleep.

A thin, blue smoke strand threaded up through the trees to the sky.

The dragonslayer.

Kaeldra knew it must be he. She squinted into the midday sky and found what she sought. A black speck, circling high above the smoke. Who else would be out in these woods with a gyrfalcon?

Hands shaking, Kaeldra untied the blanket roll. She had checked the snares as soon as she had wakened. Empty. Now the draclings thronged about her, snuffling, poking her with their noses. She meted out the last of the food, then packed to go.

⟨Hungry.⟩

⟨Hungry.⟩

⟨Hungry.⟩

⟨Not now. We must go.⟩

All afternoon the hills and ridges rose before them like waves on a wind-blown lake. Each time Kaeldra thought the next must be the last, with the Kragish Sea beyond it, a ripple of ridges would swell up before her, lapping at the horizon in long, thin lines. The shadows lengthened, and the wind whipped hard. The draclings stumbled on loose rocks and cringed against the wind, silent except for an occasional faint *hungry*, which drifted like smoke through her mind.

Kaeldra strained to hear or see the falcon, but could do neither. Yet often when she looked into the draclings' green eyes, she felt the strange floating dizziness she had sensed before. These moments filled her with foreboding, as if she could enter the draclings' minds and touch the consciousness of another—something flying—a bird. They could commune with birds, she knew, with birds and with dragon-sayers. And if a falcon could feel the draclings' thoughts, might it not lead its falconer to them?

Toward nightfall a heavy mass of clouds curled in. A late snow began to fall in fat, wet flakes.

A damp chill crept through her cloak, lodged in her bones. She strapped on her shoe-baskets, but still slipped and sank and faltered in the snow. Her feet and hands grew numb; the world shrank to a circle of snowflakes, which swarmed like sprybugs around her candle. The flame was yellow, like firelight at home. Like firelight, with something simmering—with stew in a pot above it.

When Kaeldra looked into the flame, she could feel the warmth, could hear the familiar voices, could smell the stew. She tasted the way it separated into tender strands in her mouth, the way the juices rolled over her tongue and the spices tickled her nose. She heard the baby crying. . . .

And she was in the snow again, in the freezing dark, and the kestrel was crying. She looked round for the draclings. They floundered after her, pillowed with snow. Synge lagged far behind the others and moved so slowly, Kaeldra feared she would soon collapse. There was nothing else to do. Kaeldra stumbled through the snow after Synge, then carried her in the direction of the kestrel's cry.

The wind abated; the air warmed. A darker darkness crowded around them. Trees.

Kaeldra set out the snares and made camp in the shelter of firs. Embyr and Pyro breathed sparks for a fire. There was no food.

In Kaeldra's dreams the draclings were eating. They were eating a mountain of meat.

chapter 14

Children! Obedient as hungry dragons!
     —Common parental lament, Kragrom

When Kaeldra awoke, the sun was shining. Tree boughs dripped, sloughed off snow in wet heaps. She crawled out of her snow-dusted blanket, careful not to disturb the draclings, who had burrowed in beside her.

Not far away was a vantage point where the land dropped off to the east. Kaeldra squinted into the distance, looking for a thread of smoke, a circling bird. But nothing marred the perfect blue of the sky. A bright snow-quilt spread across the shoulder of the mountain, smooth at the top, then draping and pleating below, where a tiny village nestled in its folds.

Maybe he is lost, she thought. Maybe he abandoned his pursuit and turned back.

With the sun warming her face and a village in sight, it was easy to believe that the danger was past.

There were four rabbits in the snares. Elated, Kaeldra ran back to the camping place, calling for the draclings. Embyr and Synge stumbled, yawning, from under the blanket. When they saw the rabbits, they perked up and jumped on her like puppies.

"Down! Get down, you two." She threw each a rabbit. "Pyro, you lazy oaf! Wake up!"

She poked at the rumpled blanket with her foot. Pyro did not come out. "Food, Pyro! Meat!" The blanket looked flat. Too flat. She grabbed it in one hand and yanked.

Pyro was gone.

"Pyro! Pyro, where are you?" Kaeldra fell to her knees and dug through the snow where the blanket had lain. No Pyro.

Tracks. He would have left tracks.

The snow was trampled all around, but the only tracks that led far were her own. He must have left long ago, she thought, before the snow stopped. He could be anywhere.

"Pyro!" Kaeldra wailed.

⟨Help!⟩

It was the tiniest cry, like a needleprick in her mind.

Kaeldra leaped to her feet. She scanned the forest all around; the firs were black against the snow. She ran to the bluff and looked down.

Snow and snow and trees and snow.

⟨Help!⟩

"Where *are* you?"

No answer. Kaeldra dashed back toward the camping place, then slowed, then stopped. Embyr and Synge were no longer eating. They were staring at something—staring straight up.

Kaeldra followed the direction of their gaze. Floating high in the air, caught beneath an overhanging fir bough, was Pyro.

Kaeldra's knees went weak. She had forgotten to tie them down.

"Pyro," Kaeldra said, "you come down from there."

The dracling pumped his legs futilely, like a beetle stuck on its back.

⟨Help.⟩

She couldn't climb the tree. The trunk was too wide, the lowest boughs too high. She could try to rope him or—

Kaeldra thought back to the times she had seen the draclings float in their sleep. They would rise, puffing up, as if they had taken an enormous breath. Then they would flame and shrink and drop.

"Pyro," Kaeldra said, "flame!" She closed her eyes and pictured a candle flickering in the dark.

Bright-rush!

The wet fir bough hissed; Pyro sank a little.

"Flame!"

Bright-rush!

The dracling dropped again, not far enough.

Praising and chiding by turns, Kaeldra talked him down. It was lucky that the trees were snow shrouded and did not catch fire. Gradually, Pyro took heart and even maneuvered a bit with his wings. This proved to be so much fun that he ventured higher, defying Kaeldra's commands to flame. She grabbed a rabbit and held it up high. "Look, Pyro! Meat!"

Whomp! The dracling belched out a crackling flame ball and landed with a thud upon the ground.

When they had finished eating, the kestrel called. They set off down the mountain.

The sun shone all that day. From time to time the draclings played at flying. They wobbled low over streams and gullies, pitched, reeled, rose, and dropped in jerks, then crashed—more often than not—into trees and bushes. Kaeldra tried to stop them at first, imagining them wafting away up into the sky like wyffel fluff; but finally she gave up.

By dusk they had reached the place where the forest met the fields outside the village. The draclings pestered her with their plaintive *hungry*s, and Kaeldra, too, felt weak and shaky. They skirted the fields until a low barn came into view not forty paces from the edge of the wood. A two-story stone cottage stood a little way off.

The kestrel cried and swooped down on the barn. It preened itself on the rooftop in the fading light.

⟨Stay here,⟩ Kaeldra told the draclings.

She stepped out of the wood and crept toward the barn. She tried to move soundlessly, scanning the gloom for signs of people or dogs. Yellow light seeped from cracks in the shutters of the cottage. Kaeldra hoped the people were eating, their day's work done.

The barn door was open. It was warm and dark

inside. It smelled of manure and mildew and sweet dried hay. To her right, Kaeldra could make out the cows, their backs like giant bread loaves outlined in the dark. One lowed softly. She could hear them chew. There was another animal—a mule—among them; to her left, a large mound of hay leaned against the wall.

Perhaps the kestrel meant for them to bed down here tonight. It would be soft and warm, but—there was no food here. What would they do for food?

Something tingled inside Kaeldra's head. She whipped around. Embyr peeked around the barn door.

⟨Embyr! I told you to stay! Go back!⟩

Two more dracling faces appeared. ⟨I said—⟩

But it was too late.

The cows shifted and lowed uneasily. One turned its head, saw the draclings. The rims of its eyes shone white. It let out a bellow. A cloud of hens flapped and squawked.

"Shh!" Kaeldra said to the cow. "It's all right. Just—" Another cow mooed. "Quiet!"

From somewhere outside came the slam of a door. Footsteps.

Kaeldra looked around wildly, searching for some-place to hide. The haystack. ⟨Quick! Get in here!⟩ She burrowed into the hay, the draclings fast behind her. The cows mooed and stomped. The mule brayed. A rooster crowed. Then the kestrel called, loud and long.

"Get away you, you bird!" Kaeldra heard. A boy's voice. And the sound of something pelting against the barn thatch.

The kestrel called again. It sounded thin, far away.

"Missed 'im." The boy's voice came from so close Kaeldra started. She heard him murmuring comfort to the cows, heard his footsteps on the barn floor. The sweet, musty hay smell tickled her nose. She willed herself not to sneeze; she willed the draclings to stay still.

The mule and cows calmed. The chicken squawks diminished to a disgruntled cackling. Through a gap in the straws she could make out the boy's shape as he knelt and spoke to some animals in a small hutch.

"He's gone now, little rabbits. The bad bird won't get you now."

The boy spoke to them a while longer, too softly for Kaeldra to hear. Then he crossed to the barn door. Kaeldra waited until she heard the cottage door shut, then let herself breathe again.

Food. She still had to do something about food.

She shifted around in the hay until she found all three draclings. ⟨You stay,⟩ she told them. ⟨Stay!⟩ This time she had to make them understand. They had to obey.

⟨Hungry.⟩

⟨I know you're hungry, and that's where I'm going right now. To find food. But you need to stay here. Stay! Do you understand?⟩

She felt the draclings' warm breath. It smelled like wood smoke.

⟨Well? Do you?⟩

⟨Stay.⟩ It was Embyr.

⟨That's right, Embyr. Synge?⟩

⟨Stay.⟩ The voice was a whisper in Kaeldra's mind.

⟨Good, Synge. Pyro?⟩

The hay rustled. ⟨Pyro!⟩

⟨Hungry.⟩

⟨I'll get you something to eat. Don't worry. But you have to stay. Stay.⟩

⟨Stay,⟩ Pyro grumbled.

Kaeldra sighed, unconvinced. But what more could she do?

She crawled out of the hay and brushed the clinging straws from her clothes, then stood at the barn door, watching shadows move across the shutters of the cottage.

There were people in there, and food, and a fire.

A surge of homesickness welled up inside her.

Perhaps if she knocked at the door?

But what if they asked questions? What if they had heard of her somehow? What if they could tell she wasn't a boy?

Kaeldra looked away.

Maybe there was a smokehouse. People wealthy enough to own a separate barn might have a smokehouse as well. She traced the edges of the cottage with her eyes, scanned the dark spaces on either side. Nothing. Maybe it was behind.

She walked quickly toward the cottage, alert to sounds, to movement. The moon threw her shadow across the ground. She shivered, remembering the gyrfalcon. Suddenly, atop the cottage, something moved. Kaeldra stopped, her heart pounding. She peered into the darkness.

Only the kestrel. It preened itself calmly, as if taunting the boy who thought he had chased it off. Kaeldra laughed inside herself.

And then stopped.

Inside the cottage, a dog was whining.

Shush! Kaeldra thought. Stop that!

The whining swelled to a high-pitched howl. The door banged open. Something streaked out—two things. Kaeldra tried to dodge them, but too late. A knee-high mop of fur slammed into her, knocked her down, sat on her chest. She looked up into the panting face of a shaghaired dog.

"Atta girl, Lufta!" It was a boy, the boy from the barn.

"Lufta! Get back here!" a man's voice yelled. "Gar, you let the dog out agai—" The voice stopped.

"Yanil? What is it?" A woman's voice.

Framed in the cottage doorway stood a tall man with graying hair and thick black brows, and a woman holding a baby. All around them, clinging to skirts and pant legs, were children, all manner of children: big and small, boys and girls.

They all stood there, staring.

Staring at her.

"Gar, and would you be getting our Coldran some pie?"

The boy from the barn leapt from the table, ran to the hearth.

"Let me! I want to do it! Let me!" A dark-haired

girl collided with the boy, grabbed his tunic. "Please, please, oh, please!"

Coldran was the name that had slipped into Kaeldra's mind when Yanil, the father, had asked. She had almost forgotten she was supposed to be a boy. "Kaeld—" she had said, then deepened her voice a little. "Coldran."

"I can twirl three times in the air, want to see?" another girl asked. Her hair, Kaeldra noticed, was almost as light as her own.

Kaeldra started to reply, then said "Umph," as a pudgy finger jabbed her stomach. "What's that?" demanded the finger's owner, a small boy.

Kaeldra moved her arm in front of her stomach, covering the cheese she had slipped down her tunic when no one was looking.

"Hof!" his mother said. "And will you sit down and be mindin' your manners?"

The baby in her lap sucked on its fist. "Gub!" it said happily.

Kaeldra felt bad about stealing food from these people. They had invited her to their table, fed her until she felt stuffed. They had treated her not as a stranger, but as a friend.

She looked round the room, which was larger and more richly furnished than Kaeldra's cottage. There was a stone hearth with a chimney in one corner. Oil lamps spilled golden light across pewter plates. Behind the wooden shutters, she caught a gleam of glass.

It would be nice to live here, Kaeldra thought. She wished the draclings could take care of themselves. She wished she could stay here with this family, feeling full and warm and wanted.

Something clunked on the table before her: a steaming-hot pie, bubbling with a red, sweet-smelling liquid. The boy whirled away. The dark-haired girl pouted. Across the table, the eldest girl smiled at Kaeldra, then looked quickly down at her plate.

At the front door, Lufta yipped.

"Quiet, Lufta!" Yanil said. "I don't know what's got into that cur tonight."

"She can't help it! She got bit," Gar said.

"By a wolf," one of the girls added.

"Or a dragon," another girl said.

"Gub." The baby smeared pie in its hair.

"No such thing as dragons," Gar said.

"Says who?"

"Says me!"

"That man said so." The dark-haired girl turned to Yanil. "The apothecary man. Didn't he, Da?"

"So what does he know?" Gar said. "He never even saw one. He just said—"

"Children!" Yanil's voice cut through the bickering. He glared at them from beneath his bristling eyebrows, although a touch of amusement flickered at the corner of his mouth as he turned to Kaeldra.

She wanted to ask about the apothecary, but Yanil spoke first. "So you're bound for Kragrom, are you?"

"I'm to be apprenticed," Kaeldra said. "To a black-smith my grandmother knows there." She listened to the lie as she said it, to see if it sounded true.

116

"What's that?" Hof asked, tugging at her coin purse.

Kaeldra smiled and gently detached his fingers from the purse.

"I'll be goin' that way myself," Yanil continued. "Well, not all the way to Kragrom, but I'll be cartin' some brew to Regalch, by the Kragish Sea. You could bide a night or two with us, couldn't you? And ride with me as far as Regalch? I could book you on a vessel bound for Kragrom. It'd be a boon to have another man along."

Kaeldra gaped, so astonished she couldn't think what to say.

"Yes, please stay," the eldest girl said. She smiled, raised her eyelashes, then lowered them again. With a jolt, Kaeldra recognized her look. It was the kind of look that Mirym exchanged with Wynn. A private look. A girl-to-boy look. Kaeldra gulped and took a spoonful of pie.

"What's that?" Hof was reaching for her hood. Horrified, Kaeldra felt it begin to slide off her head.

"I can dance the jeika, want to see?"

"The man said—"

"Did not!"

"Quiet, Lufta!"

"Gub!"

The smile froze on the eldest girl's face. Yanil's spoon stopped halfway to his mouth. Even the dog was quiet.

Kaeldra grabbed for her hood, but too late.

"He's a *girl*!" Hof said.

"I—" Kaeldra choked. The words stuck in her throat. She groped for something credible to say, some-

117

thing to explain why a boy would wear his hair in a braid, or else why a girl would pass herself off as a boy. Dimly, she heard a squawking of hens, a mooing of cows, the braying of a mule. At the table, no one moved.

Suddenly, the kestrel screamed. The dog set up a frenzy of barking and scratching. The cows were bellowing now; the hens screeched.

"What in the name of—" Yanil jumped up and ran to the door. There was a scraping of benches, a pounding of feet.

Squeezing into the doorway, children crowded all around her, Kaeldra saw the draclings.

They were flying.

They drifted, wobbling, through the air, then flamed down at three panicked rabbits. Embyr flopped down on one, then dragged it wriggling and kicking along the ground. Pyro missed, landed snoot-first in the dirt, lunged, and heaved himself down upon a rabbit.

"By the sun's blessed rays," Yanil whispered.

Kaeldra's legs refused to move. She willed them to go, but they wouldn't. Then the kestrel called again, and she was pushing past the family, she was out in the barnyard.

"Flee!" she shouted to the draclings.

"Flee!"

chapter 15

He who tasteth of power
Weaker fare will nevermore content.

—Kragish proverb

Kaeldra ran.

There was a commotion behind her, shoutings and squawkings and barkings. "Stay here," Kaeldra heard, and, "Grab the dog."

"Come on!" she yelled at the draclings. She made for the woods at the far side of the clearing. The draclings loped along beside her, limp rabbits hanging from their mouths.

"Run!"

They were halfway across the clearing when the dog's frustrated yips changed to furious barking.

"Fly!" Kaeldra screamed. "Drop those stupid rabbits and fly!"

But the draclings would not let go of their prey.

Kaeldra looked over her shoulder to see the dog hurtling across the field, narrowing the gap between them to a tiny strip of dirt. Synge had fallen behind; the dog made for her and leaped.

"Synge! Drop it! Fly!"

But it was too late. The dog landed on Synge's back. Synge let out a scream. Pain ripped through Kaeldra's shoulder. Synge's pain, she thought. Not mine.

Kaeldra turned and ran toward the dog. "Stop that! Stop! Go home!"

But the dog, though not large, was determined. Snarling, it buried its teeth into the dracling's soft shoulder-scales. Synge whipped at it with her tail, screamed pitifully, rolled over on the ground. A swarm of birds converged overhead, swooped at the dog. The dog hung on. Synge twisted and flailed and lashed her tail. Still the dog hung on.

Synge was weakening, Kaeldra saw. A bright red stain trickled down her foreleg. Her screams diminished to soft whimperings. Her tail flopped to the ground, lifted, hit down again with a thud. It lay on the ground, quivering.

No, Kaeldra thought. This can't be. This can't be happening. She flung herself at the dog, dug her nails into its fur, tried to pry it off Synge. The birds were diving, pecking at the dog. Still, it hung on. She pummeled it with her fists; it twisted savagely, bit Kaeldra's arm, then again sank its teeth into Synge.

Kaeldra cried out. She clutched at her arm, slid away

from the dog. Blood seeped up between her fingers from an evil-looking gash.

Embyr and Pyro pawed at the ground, snorted smoke, twitched their heads as if shaking off bees.

"Do something!" Kaeldra sobbed. "Attack! Bite!" She reached to touch them with her mind and felt a paralyzing confusion of pain and fear and rage.

She jumped to her feet.

⟨Flame!⟩

The draclings stared.

Kaeldra closed her eyes. In her mind she called up a candle. The wick blossomed into flame. She focused on the flame. Shadows blew across it, tried to distract her, tried to snuff it out. The dog snarling. The voices calling. Someone running toward her across the field. Kaeldra held fast to the flame.

⟨Flame oh flame oh please please flame.⟩

Bright-rush!

The dog howling. The stench of burning fur. Kaeldra opened her eyes, saw the dog drop down, then leap again for Synge.

Kaphoom!

Rearing up on hind legs, necks arched, nostrils flaring, Embyr and Pyro breathed fire. Blue flame shot through the air and engulfed the dog, then tumbled across the damp field, hissing and smoking until it fizzled at last at the forest's edge. The dog was gone. Where it had stood only a moment before, a black, mangled heap lay smoking on the ground. There was a nauseating stench of charred flesh and burning fur.

Kaeldra's stomach heaved. *They killed it. They truly killed the dog.*

She tore her eyes away from the smoking carcass and ran to Synge. The flame seemed not to have touched the dracling, but her shoulder oozed blood.

Kaeldra was bending to comfort Synge when the rock hit her back.

"Ouch!" Kaeldra whirled around.

"They killed my dog! They killed my rabbits! I hate them!"

It was Gar, the boy. He stood not three cart-lengths away, fists clenched, eyes filled with tears. Across the field, people were shouting and running toward them.

Embyr and Pyro reared again, faced the boy.

⟨No,⟩ Kaeldra said to the draclings. Her bloodbeat rang loud in her ears. ⟨No. Absolutely do not. No.⟩

The draclings glanced at her, and her mind was flooded with a churning agitation, a powerful urge to breathe fire.

The draclings looked back at Gar. Their nostrils flared. Gar froze, his eyes widening.

Kaeldra walked slowly to the boy, careful to do nothing to startle them. "Stand still," she whispered. She moved in front of Gar and reached back to hold his trembling hands. Dimly she was aware that the people had stopped. They, too, stood frozen, as if afraid to move.

Staring at Embyr and Pyro, Kaeldra made a picture in her mind. They were in the woods, eating their rabbits. The meat was tender and juicy.

Pyro dipped his head. Slowly, with the grace of a

cat, he lowered his talons to the ground. He picked up his kill and made for the woods.

But Embyr reared up higher. Smoke billowed out her nostrils.

⟨No, Embyr. No.⟩ Embyr glared back at Kaeldra, and she knew from the look in the dragon's wild eyes that Embyr was no longer hers to command. Embyr would do as she pleased, and Kaeldra could only watch.

A cold wind gusted against Kaeldra's back. The dragon's tail twitched.

Then Embyr slowly lowered herself to the ground.

Kaeldra let out a breath. She picked up Synge's kill and followed the draclings into the woods.

Behind her, she could hear Gar sob.

It was raining.

Drops slapped against the dense tree roof. One escaped through the branches, splashed cold on Kaeldra's head.

She huddled on a soggy stump while the draclings tore and gulped their prey. She averted her eyes, trying not to think of how horribly the dog had died and how nearly the boy had met the same fate.

The dog attacked them, Kaeldra told herself. And they *didn't* kill the boy.

Still, something had changed. She felt a new awe for her charges and, mingled with it, fear.

Kaeldra's arm throbbed painfully. She had bound it and Synge's shoulder with rags torn from the bottom edge of her tunic, but already both wounds had bled through.

123

She had thought it safe to stop since it was past sundown, and she had heard no one following. The searchers would likely wait until dawn.

But there would be searchers. Of that, she felt sure.

Pyro licked his mouth and sucked at his talons, savoring the last trace of meat. Soon Embyr and Synge had finished as well.

High above, the kestrel called.

⟨Let's go,⟩ Kaeldra said.

A thick, white mist curled about the tree trunks. The kestrel called often, muted, as though wrapped in wool. Kaeldra could not see the bird and so felt her way toward its sound along narrow animal tracks or through sodden underbrush. After a time she gave up listening for the kestrel, for the draclings moved infallibly toward its call.

Soon, her boots and stockings were soaked. Damp soaked into her tunic; cold seeped in through her skin to her bones. She had left everything at the cottage—her cloak, her blanket, her snares, her food—everything but her coin purse, which was tied to her belt. She had no idea which way they traveled—whether the kestrel still led them toward the Kragish Sea or simply away.

At last they came to a clearing, where stood a run-down, half-timbered building. Amber light leaked from its windows, illuminating silvery needles of rain. Drawing closer, Kaeldra saw a sign hanging above the door.

An inn. It must be an inn.

She reached down to touch her coin purse. At least she still had that. She did not know how much a night at an inn would cost, but it couldn't be more than what Granmyr had given her. There would be a fire and blankets and a bed.

Synge nudged her hand. Her bandage was bloody and dark. She must hurt, Kaeldra thought. Her own arm throbbed from the dog bite, but Synge's wound was worse.

She took a last, longing look at the inn. ⟨Come on.⟩

They followed the kestrel around the edge of the clearing to where a muddy road passed by the inn. Several carts clustered there. Their horses were gone; the inn must have a stable.

The kestrel preened itself atop one of the carts. It was an odd conveyance, completely enclosed like a large lidded box. Faded red paint peeled off in flakes, giving it the look of a man too long in the sun.

Perhaps the kestrel meant for them to go inside. They would be out of the wet and hidden from searchers. If the owner had stopped at the inn . . .

Kaeldra tiptoed to the front of the cart. The draclings skulked at her heels. Slowly, she pulled herself onto the carter's bench. It creaked. The draclings scrambled under the cart.

Silence.

Kaeldra turned and peered inside.

It was dark at first, too dark to see. But the smells wrapped around her like a cloak. Ringboll and tinewort, the smell of wet fur. Axle grease, picklefish, pond scum, and smoke. There were smells that pricked at the edges

125

of her memory; there were smells she had never smelled before.

Kaeldra hesitated. What kind of cart was this?

As her eyes adjusted to the dark, she saw that the cart was narrower inside than it had appeared from without. No one seemed to be in it, although she could make out a lumpy pile on the floor in back. Kaeldra moved into the cart, groped her way toward the pile. Gingerly, she touched it.

Blankets. A straw mat.

The carter must be staying at the inn.

It was a strange place, but a dry one, and the kestrel had chosen it.

⟨Come,⟩ she called.

The draclings slunk into the cart. Kaeldra spread out the blankets, crawled onto the mat. The draclings burrowed in beside her.

Just for a while, Kaeldra thought. I'll wake before daybreak, before the carter returns.

On the roof, rain softly drummed. Nestled close, the draclings thrummed.

The ground was moving.

It lurched beneath her, jolting her awake. There was a clattering racket, a hubbub of rattles and jingles and clinks.

Kaeldra opened her eyes.

The walls were moving. Jiggling. No, not the walls, but an astonishing jumble of bottles and jars on shelves. Floor to ceiling. Front to back.

126

The ground lurched again, and they leapt into the air, then clanked down hard.

The cart! It was moving. She was still in the cart, and the cart was moving.

Kaeldra sat up. She checked to make sure all three draclings were there, sleeping beneath the blanket, then turned to the front of the cart. On the driver's bench a man in a faded tunic slouched in the morning sunlight.

What kind of cart *was* this?

A crude, wooden lip at the edge of each shelf kept the jars from falling off. Kaeldra plucked a green ceramic jar from a shelf near her, turned it round in her hands. It smelled ripe and rank, like decaying things in a bog. In a purple glass bottle behind the jar, a huge floating eyeball leered at her.

Ugh! Kaeldra shoved the green jar back onto the shelf.

Beneath the blanket, a dracling stirred.

⟨Shhh! Be still!⟩

A twinge of fear. ⟨Still?⟩ It was Synge.

⟨Yes. You must not move.⟩

⟨Still?⟩ This was Embyr.

⟨Yes, Embyr. Still. Or we will be caught.⟩

She felt a low complaining rumble, then a relaxing into sleep. She must have decided to obey me, Kaeldra thought, relieved. For now.

Kaeldra pondered what to do. The jars and bottles clanked.

"Well! I see you're up!"

Beneath the blanket, the draclings started.

127

⟨Still! Be still!⟩

She turned to the front of the cart.

The man was looking at her.

His face was round and leathery. Black curls sprang out in all directions from his head.

"Come on out. I saved you breakfast."

chapter 16

For the breaking of a bladder stone:
Tayke one gallipot of dragon's blood and mingle
therein the juice of seven pommefruits. Strayne
through fine-woven cloth and let stand in a warm
place. Quaff therefrom until the brew is wholly drunk,
or until one moon-turn has passed.

—*Bok of Medik*

Did he see the draclings?

Kaeldra clutched the shelf edges as she made her
way to the front of the cart.

Is he angry that I slept here? Does he know who I
am?

She moved slowly, trying to gather her thoughts,
trying to plan what to say; but her mind would not focus.

As she crawled onto the carter's bench, the man
thrust something into her hands. A bread roll, split, with
a slab of meat inside.

"Here," he said. He was smiling. "Your breakfast."

"Thank you." Kaeldra sat on the bench, still holding

the roll. The day was bright and warm. Pulled by two ancient, swaybacked nags, the cart traveled along a rutted road through a meadow ringed with mountains and firs.

"Go ahead!" the man said. "Don't be shy! I already ate mine. They gave me more than I needed at the inn, so I brought some back with me. When I saw you, I said to myself, 'Hokarth,' I said, 'there's a fellow needs it more than you.'" He chuckled and patted his ample belly.

"Thank you," Kaeldra said again. She took a bite. The meat was spicy and still warm. The juices had soaked into the bread. It was wonderful.

"Good?" the man asked.

Kaeldra nodded.

"I thought you'd like that. Nothing beats a slab of roast beef for breakfast, I always say. Unless it's a hot kidney pie."

"Um hmm." Kaeldra swallowed, turned to the man. He had big brown eyes that crinkled at the corners. His curly black hair was matted down in some places and stuck out in others. His clothes were tattered and patched.

"I'm sorry I—ah—slept in your cart last night," Kaeldra began. "I lost my blanket roll yesterday. I was going to stay only a few hours, but—"

The man waved his hand. "Don't worry about it. I've been down on my luck a few times myself. Besides, I'm a family man. You remind me of a son of mine."

"A son!" Kaeldra choked, remembering suddenly that she was supposed to be a boy. She reached up to check her hood. It was in place.

"Yes, a son! Seven sons and five daughters I've got, officially, that is, and three or four whelps on the side." He winked at Kaeldra. "Ah, the ladies. You know how it is. But one day a son of mine could be wearing your boots, if you know what I mean, and I'd be grateful if someone offered him breakfast."

"Well—I—um, thank you," Kaeldra said, feeling stupid.

"By the way, I'm Hokarth, apothecary extraordinaire, at your service." He bowed with a flourish. "And you are . . ."

"Uh, Styfan," Kaeldra said. "I'm on my way to my uncle to be his apprentice."

"You're welcome to come along with me as far as you're going. Which is . . .?"

"Ah—Regalch."

"Regalch! I'm headed that way, too. Got to make a few stops on the way—business, you know—but you could come along, just be a few days, maybe lend a hand?"

A few days! Kaeldra had had no idea Regalch was so far. A few days with the draclings inside the cart was impossible. But she could think of no polite way to refuse, so she nodded and took another bite of her meat.

"Galloping gallstones, what's that!" Kaeldra whirled back toward the cart, toward the draclings. But Hokarth was looking at her arm. In the daylight, the blood-soaked rag looked worse than she had realized.

"Oh, that. It's all right. I was bitten by a dog."

"It's all right! It's all right, he says! No, it is *not* all right. All kinds of things can happen with a wound like

131

that if it's not properly treated." Hokarth maneuvered the cart to the side of the road and stopped. He turned to go inside.

"Wait!" Kaeldra said, terrified that the draclings might have crept out from beneath the blanket, or were floating in their sleep. But Hokarth was already in the cart.

"It won't hurt," his voice came, "*unless* you wait. Come on!"

Kaeldra stepped inside. The blankets seemed huge and lumpy, seemed to cry out that something was amiss. But the draclings were still, at least. She felt a questioning and knew that it was Embyr. ⟨It's all right,⟩ she said, trying to calm the dracling's mind.

Hokarth did not seem to notice the blankets. He wiggled his fingers around the motley collection of jars and bottles, muttering, "Let me see now, I know it's here, it's, no, it's over—aha!" He reached for a squat ceramic jar. "I knew it was there! Let me see that arm."

He unwrapped the cloth. Kaeldra flinched when he came to the last layer; it pulled painfully away from her skin. "Hmm," the apothecary said, looking at the wound. "Not as bad as it could be. Good thing I'm getting to it now."

He uncorked the jar and shook a yellowish powder into a small stone bowl. Then he poured in a bright green liquid and mixed them together into a paste. The cart now reeked, a putrid, stomach-turning smell, like something gone to rot.

Hokarth spread the concoction over Kaeldra's arm. It instantly felt cooler, better.

"What is it?" Kaeldra asked.

"Powdered salamander jaws and swamp water. The best there is for dog bites." He finished spreading the stuff on Kaeldra's arm and wiped his hands on his tunic. "Though nothing's perfect, if you want the truth. You promise them miracles, then you leave town and hope they're cured by the time you get back." Hokarth crammed the jars onto the shelves—but not where he had found them. "Unless, of course, you can lay your hands on some dragon fat, which is a steed of a different breed, I can tell you."

Kaeldra jumped. *"What?"*

"Dragon fat." Hokarth wagged a stumpy finger at her. "Oh, you don't believe in dragons, I can see that. You're a modern lad, believe only what you see." He rummaged through the shelves, pulling out bottles, apparently looking for something. "Time was, a man could hardly poach a hart without sticking a dragon by mistake. But there still be dragons about, though a good deal rarer than before. You get yourself some dragon fat, you soak it in olive oil for seven days. Then you boil it in vinegar and strain it through a sieve—where is that thing? You cool it in the nocturnal air and then—wait a minute. I think it's—" He turned and began fumbling around on the other side of the cart. "Rub it on morning and night, and—aha! I knew it was here!" Triumphant, he pulled out a roll of loose-woven cloth. "This wound would be healed in, say, a day and a half."

"Oh," Kaeldra said. Suddenly she felt weak. She caught a sudden movement out of the corner of her eye. The blanket was shifting, thrashing about.

133

⟨Still! Be still!⟩

"What would I not give for a dead dragon!" Hokarth was saying. He shook his head wistfully, then tore off a strip of cloth. He began to wrap it around Kaeldra's arm. "Why, the bones alone, when ground to a fine powder, will cure migraines, creeping ulcers, and the infirmities of pregnant women. The teeth are good for gallstones and the palsy. Turn your arm this way, please. The tongue, liver, and bladder wipe out night-visions and liver spots. For snake bites and fever, you take a pair of dragon eyes, beat them into a froth. You put them in a pot with milk and red wine, and—are you feeling all right?"

Kaeldra nodded, but she was not. Her stomach lurched wildly; the draclings made a roaring and a hurting in her mind.

From under the blanket, a head appeared. ⟨Embyr! Get back!⟩

Quickly, Kaeldra moved to face the rear of the cart so that Hokarth was forced to turn his back to the draclings.

"And the blood!" The apothecary rolled his eyes, continuing to wrap Kaeldra's arm. "Talk to me not of dragon's blood." Behind him, Embyr snorted out a smoke-puff, turned around, and burrowed beneath the blanket. But not all the way. Poking out beyond one edge was the tip of a green-scaled tail.

"Blindness, kidney stones, madness, gout," Hokarth went on, "it's a panacea. Of course, you have to know what you're doing. You cool the fat at the wrong time of day or mix things in the wrong proportions—" He shook his head, clucking his tongue. "Disaster."

"It—must be very difficult," Kaeldra said faintly. The tail tip swished. Kaeldra swallowed.

"Difficult! Talk to me not of difficult! This is art! I tell you in all modesty that no more than one person in a thousand has the talent to work these things. But who appreciates it? No one."

The apothecary sighed. He tied the ends of the cloth and looked absently at his handiwork. "But with a dragon—with a dragon I could do such things as even a king would sit up and take note of." He sighed again, glanced up at Kaeldra. "You *are* peaked. I'll get you something. Let me see, where is that potion, it's—" He reached toward the back of the cart.

"No!" Kaeldra grabbed his arm. "I'm fine, truly I am. I only need, ah, some fresh air."

Hokarth chuckled. "I forgot, you're not used to the aroma. Well, come on, then. We'll be on our way."

They rode through most of the day. The draclings' agitation soon calmed; they slept for hours. Thrice Kaeldra caught sight of the kestrel flying ahead.

The land gentled around them as they rode. Steep mountain ridges gave way to rolling fields, interspersed with brakes of oak and larin and elm. This was lowland terrain, a softer, warmer land than Elythia. They passed by many travelers, but no one seemed to be searching for Kaeldra.

Toward supper time, they came to a village. Hokarth pulled up by a tavern. He asked if Kaeldra would go with him to sup, but she declined, saying she was tired. If he would just bring her something . . . He left, promising to return soon.

It was yet light. Carts drew up and departed; men entered and left the tavern. Kaeldra slipped inside the cart; the draclings thronged about her, thrumming.

⟨Hungry,⟩ Pyro said.

"I know. We will wait until dark, until Hokarth sleeps, and then we will go. We will find something then." Kaeldra didn't know what they would find, or how. She was surprised that the draclings had stayed quiet for so long. Soon, she feared, they would become unmanageable.

⟨Hurt,⟩ Synge whined.

Kaeldra removed the bloody rag and examined the wound. It had stopped bleeding, but was swollen and oozed a yellowish fluid. She wished she could remember which jars Hokarth had used to mix the poultice for her own arm. Perhaps leaving the wound exposed to the air would help.

She scratched Synge's eye ridges; before long the draclings burrowed beneath the blankets. Kaeldra lay beside them, listened to the quiet whistle of their breath in sleep.

She woke with a dizzy feeling, as though the ground had fallen away beneath her. Her head floated and spun. She had felt this way before, she knew, but, half-asleep, could not place it.

Ill, she thought. I must truly be ill.

Kaeldra sat up. The draclings were tense, alert.

⟨Be still.⟩ Embyr's voice. Talking to *her*.

Kaeldra strained her ears in the darkness; then she heard it. A crunching noise outside the cart.

A footstep?

Just then the tavern noise swelled, receded. There was laughing, and footsteps, definitely footsteps. Someone was coming this way.

Hokarth's voice, talking to the nag. Then another voice, very near.

Kaeldra's scalp prickled. Now she remembered the dizzy feeling, the feeling of flight: the gyrfalcon. The voice brought it back.

Jeorg Sigrad's voice.

". . . traveling alone," he said. "About yea high, with straw-colored hair. Have you seen her?"

"No." The apothecary sounded different, somehow. Abrupt. Agitated.

"I, uh, heard someone was riding with you in your cart this afternoon."

"Then you heard wrong. I've been alone all day. Now I'll be going." The cart dipped and creaked as the apothecary climbed onto the bench. There was the crack of a whip, and the cart jerked forward.

She was trembling. Kaeldra didn't realize it until after they had left. He was here, and he knew, somehow, that she had been in the cart. The apothecary had lied; she had gotten away—for now—but for some reason that didn't make Kaeldra feel any better. There was something about Hokarth—his voice. . . .

I'll pretend to be asleep, Kaeldra thought. He has

to sleep sometime, and then we'll slip away.

After a time the cart slowed and came to a stop. The driver's bench creaked; Kaeldra heard Hokarth moving into the cart.

"Psst! he said.

Kaeldra pretended to sleep.

"Psst! Hey! You! Wake up!" He shook her shoulders.

"Um, what?" Kaeldra blinked. A blinding bright light shone into her eyes. Hokarth's brew-and-onions breath filled her nose.

The light moved away. A candle, Kaeldra saw.

"They are," Hokarth said.

"What? What are?"

"Green. Your eyes are green."

Kaeldra felt the fear rise inside her, fill her throat. Hokarth touched her hair, then suddenly yanked down her hood. "A girl," he said. "You're the girl. You're the dragon girl they spoke of in the tavern. The one they're searching for."

The apothecary's bloodshot eyes stared at her with a strange intensity. Kaeldra moved away. She wanted to deny it, to cry out that he was wrong, but the words stuck fast.

"Where are they?" he asked.

"What? Where are what?" Kaeldra pushed the words up out of her throat.

"Come on, girl! The dragons. Where are they?"

"I don't—I don't know. What dragons? What—"

The apothecary shook her again, saying, "Don't you understand what this means to me? To us! Us! This is our chance, don't you see?"

138

Something bright and burning sliced through her mind. She winced and closed her eyes. ⟨Be still,⟩ she said. ⟨Please. He doesn't know you are here.⟩

When she opened her eyes, Hokarth was smiling. He was smiling at her with his mouth, but his eyes looked wild.

"We could be rich," he said. "You and I. With those dragons, we could be rich. I have the art. They would welcome us as honored guests. They would *beg* us to come. They would respect my art. And they would pay— oh, they would pay."

His voice took on a wheedling tone. "I'm just a family man," he said. "I only want respect and a few simple pleasures." The smile dropped off his face. He leaned in close to Kaeldra, gripping her shoulders so hard it hurt.

"Please," he whined. "I *need* those dragons."

She heard them in her head. Their fear clattered and rang against her skull, so loud she thought surely he must hear. And then the blanket was moving and the draclings were there, rearing up, necks arched. "No!" Kaeldra screamed. She threw herself at Hokarth; together they hit the floor. Flame poured above them, scorched her hair, drenched the cart in light.

She scrambled to get out, the draclings fast behind. They tumbled to the ground and ran for the woods. Behind her she heard Hokarth shouting, "Wait! Don't go! Hear me out!"

The explosion knocked her flat. She tried to get up, but the ground shuddered and darkness rushed in.

chapter 17

Mayke you a slit in the serpent's belly; tayke out its entrails and stuff with sour-fruit and scallions. Scoop out of the earth a pit and lay thereon a bed of coals. Pat the serpent with wet clay; set it in the pit. Cover with earth and mayke a fire on it. When four days have passed, unearth the serpent and crack open the clay.

—Ancient Kragish recipe

The draclings were gone.

She felt their absence first, and then, opening her eyes, scanned the darkness. A wall of trees loomed before her; behind, across a clearing, a fire smoldered.

No draclings.

Kaeldra closed her eyes again and tried to think back, tried to remember how she came to be here, on the ground, in the dark, all alone. But her thoughts leaped about like the shadows of a bonfire; they would not be still.

She sat up. There was a tinkling sound. A rill of glass shards shivered down her back. Glass littered the ground, glittered in the moonlight.

Her hands hurt. Looking down, Kaeldra saw that they were riddled with tiny cuts. She picked out the largest slivers of glass then got to her feet, shaking out her clothes and hair. Glass cascaded about her in a glittering spume.

What had happened?

Memory flared: draclings flaming, an explosion.

Explosion. Just like— The thought stopped her heart.

Fiora. Fiora had exploded, too.

She moved toward the cart, dread seeping into her chest, glass crunching beneath her boots. Smoke rose from the wreckage; charred wood spiked up from it. She could not tell what was there and what was not. She needed to look under things; she needed to move things.

Kaeldra ran to a tree and broke off a low branch, then raked through the wood, through the potsherds, through the bright, brittle rivers of glass.

The draclings had teeth. She found no teeth.

The draclings had bones. She found no bones.

Her hands went limp; the branch dropped to the ground. "Thank the heavens!" she whispered. She sank down with a crunch, tried to piece together the fragments of her thoughts.

An explosion. And before that, the draclings had flamed. And before that, the apothecary had found out about the draclings. And before that—the dragonslayer.

Kaeldra shivered. Where were the draclings now? Where was Hokarth? His nags were gone, she saw; their

141

hoof prints led into the wood. Had he pursued the draclings? Had he captured them? And the kestrel—where was it?

Kaeldra looked up, searched for its shape in the tree branches.

It was gone. They all were gone. Perhaps—the thought came to her unbidden—perhaps she might go home.

"Home." She said it aloud and felt a sudden lightness, as if a burden had been lifted from her back. She had wanted—it hurt to admit it—she had wanted to be free of the draclings. She didn't want to be the dragon girl. It would be so easy now to go home, home to Lyf and Mirym and Granmyr.

Perhaps, Kaeldra thought hopefully, the kestrel would lead the draclings to Rog. They could hunt now, a little. They had fire.

But there were wolves and hunters and bands of angry farmers. There was the apothecary. There was the dragonslayer. The draclings might be captives, even now.

Above the trees the waxing moon hovered. Far off, she heard a ring owl's lonely cry. Inside her, there was a silent place, once filled with talk and dracling thoughts.

Kaeldra leaped up. ⟨Embyr! Pyro! Synge!⟩

In her listening mind she felt it, a faint tingling. ⟨Where are you? Embyr!⟩

A cry, high and distant. A kestrel's cry. She heard a growing, rapid wingbeat and then the cry again, louder this time. The kestrel burst through the trees. Thrice it circled the clearing, then disappeared into the wood.

Kaeldra followed, pushed through the underbrush in the direction it had gone. At last, scratched and weary, she spied the bird preening on the bole of an enormous uprooted oak. In the cage formed by its roots she made out three huddled shapes.

The draclings. Kaeldra let out a slow breath and, creeping closer, saw that they were trembling. They stared at her with wild, frightened eyes. But why?

⟨Why are you afraid?⟩ she asked. ⟨Is Hokarth near?⟩

She reached to touch Embyr's mind and felt a burst of light, a blistering shudder of sound.

The explosion. It must have terrified them. The last time they had felt an explosion, they had lost their mother. This time they must have believed they had lost Kaeldra.

"Hey," Kaeldra whispered, reaching her hand between the roots for the draclings to sniff. "I'm here."

Tentatively, Embyr sniffed Kaeldra's hand. Then the draclings squeezed out from between the roots. They crowded onto her lap, flicked their tongues, nuzzled her face. Their breath was smoky and warm. Kaeldra laughed, and the sound of it burst inside her, made her throat catch and her eyelids sting.

The next morning Kaeldra made a breakfast of roasted acorns for herself and the draclings. Then they set off through the wood after the kestrel. Their progress was slow, for the trees, massive oaks and blackwood, were knit with tangled skeins of nectarvine and parse-bramble and ivy.

Only slivers of sky showed behind the thickly layered branches, but the slivers seemed brighter in the direction they faced. We must be traveling east, Kaeldra thought, toward the sea. Though she kept a sharp eye out, she saw no sign of Hokarth; nor did she see any bird resembling a gyrfalcon. Still, she could not feel easy in her mind, especially when she thought of what lay ahead. How ever would she get the draclings across the Kragish Sea?

During the day the air was warm, redolent of moss and blooms and sweet new growth. Kaeldra gathered corberries and lichelroots and hoarnuts to eat; the draclings flipped fish from a stream. But at night the cold crawled up from the ground and clung to Kaeldra's back.

On the third day they came to a river, and on the fifth, the river crossed a narrow dirt track. The kestrel led them along the track; Kaeldra watched and listened for signs of other travelers so that the draclings might hide. But they met none. Late that day they emerged from the forest, and there was a town—wall and rooftops—sprawled out on the land before them. Behind the town stood a castle with tiny rounded towers and bright banners, which fluttered gaily in the breeze. And behind the castle was water, stretching away to the edges of the sky.

"Regalch," Kaeldra breathed. "This must be Regalch."

But now she was more worried than before. Never had she imagined that a sea could be so vast. How *would* she get the draclings across it?

They skirted the forest so as not to be seen, until it ended at a bluff above the sea. There they waited for dark. Then the kestrel led them down a treacherous path, which twisted and turned across the bluff face, then plunged at last into a cave.

The draclings settled down quickly for the night. But Kaeldra stayed awake, gazing across the vast, moonlit sea, breathing hard against the despair that weighed upon her heart.

The next morning she knew what she must do. She still had the coins Granmyr had given her; she must hire a mule cart and purchase a tarp for the draclings to hide beneath. Then she must book passage on a ship bound for Rog. It was, Kaeldra felt, a flawed plan—a bad plan in fact—but it was all that she could think of.

The draclings were asleep, back from a nighttime foray. Kaeldra had awakened in the middle of the night to find them gone and, when she had called, had felt them returning from somewhere deep inside the cave. Now she saw that they bulged about their middles as though they had eaten something. A slimy film coated their scales, and they smelled of rot. Kaeldra peered uneasily into the cavern, but felt no desire to explore. Anyway, she told herself, she had no candles.

⟨Stay,⟩ Kaeldra said, crouching beside Embyr, trying not to inhale too deeply.

Embyr tilted up her chin and opened a sleepy eye.

⟨Stay here, Embyr. It is not safe outside the cave. I'll soon return.⟩

Embyr closed her eye and thrummed noncommittally.

145

If I hurry, Kaeldra thought, I'll be back before they wake.

Kaeldra slipped through the town gates in a mob of travelers and pack mules and gabbling geese. Inside, shops and houses bunched together like sheep in a shearing pen. The air smelled of sea brine and dead fish and things she didn't know. No longer did the castle seem small; it had grown as she approached until it filled the eastern sky.

She wandered through the cobbled streets, wondering how to buy a cart or book passage on a ship. People bustled about, all seeming in a hurry to get someplace important. Kaeldra noticed with surprise that many were taller than she, and some were fairer of skin and hair. Their garments were vibrant-hued—scarlet and purple, teal and gold—unlike the muted pastels of Elythia. Self-conscious, Kaeldra ran her hand over the rags—boy's rags—she wore. The fabric was stiff and coarse and sticky with sap.

A carter creaked past, hauling a load of yellow squamkins. "Excuse me, sir?" Kaeldra began, approaching. "Could you tell me—"

"Off with you, ragrat!" the carter said, shaking his whip at her. "Git!"

Kaeldra shrank away, blinking back the tears that stung her eyes. A pox on Granmyr! How did she expect Kaeldra to get those draclings across the Kragish Sea? She didn't know how. She couldn't do it. *Couldn't.*

She blundered toward the far end of town with the vague notion of finding a harbor gate, and thence a ship.

146

Before long she found herself amidst a throng of people milling about before a huge, barred gate, flanked by two stone towers. A few stray gulls hopped and pecked on the battlements.

But this was the castle gate, not the harbor gate. Kaeldra turned to go. Just then there was a grating noise, and the gulls fluttered, screeching, into the sky. The gate was rising. A sudden shout; hoofbeats clattered. Kaeldra was shoved to one side by a tide of human bodies.

And not a moment too soon. A troop of horsemen burst from between the shops behind Kaeldra and pounded across the ramp. Through the crowd she saw brief flashes of color: a gold banner, a red cloak, a blur of faces.

Again Kaeldra tried to escape, but too late. The mob surged forward, dragging her with it. She was jostled and shoved and stepped on; the air reeked with the musk of human sweat. The castle wall moved close, surrounded her, then disappeared behind her shoulders.

She was inside the castle. She must get out! She had already been gone too long; if she were caught in here, the draclings would become restless and who knew what they would do!

Kaeldra turned and pushed against the mob, but the grating sound came again, and the gate slid down and crashed against the cobblestones.

She was trapped.

Now the crowd thinned and dissipated. Kaeldra stood at the edge of an enormous, cobblestoned court-yard, bordered by thatch-roofed buildings, which hugged the castle walls. Grooms helped the horsemen dismount and led their mounts to a stable. A blacksmith clanged at his forge. Armored sentries scurried about.

"Hey, you!"

Something hard jabbed at her side. A man in leathers prodded her with the butt end of his spear.

"Off, pig swill!"

"But I need to go out—"

The man made as if to jab her again. "Get where you belong!"

I don't belong anywhere, she thought. I am like the draclings; there is no place for me. I am *farin*, no matter where I go.

Kaeldra stumbled away from the sentry and headed for a place far across the courtyard where a knot of stragglers were disappearing through a stone-arched doorway.

It was the biggest room she had ever seen. It was like being outdoors. The ceiling reached for the sky in overlapping arches. There was a din of talk, a hubbub of workers, and an overwhelming aroma of food.

Abruptly, Kaeldra realized she had eaten almost nothing but berries and nuts for many days. Her mouth began to water as she watched blackened carcasses turn on spits in enormous fire pits. Across the room, a man was carving a huge, charred hunk of meat. The slices fell away, thin and pink and juicy. Workers piled them onto platters, then vanished through another arched doorway at the far end of the room.

Kaeldra edged toward the meat, past a row of troughs, past a square hole in the floor into which a boy tossed a bucketful of peelings. Steam wafted from the meat in an aromatic cloud. She reached for a small chunk that had fallen onto the table.

"Oh, no you don't!"

A hand clamped onto Kaeldra's wrist, and she was dragged across the room behind a stout, hooded figure.

Near a low trough her captor stopped. "Know you not the penalty for stealing the lord's meat?" she hissed.

It was a woman, broad faced, snub-nosed. One of her front teeth was missing, and the edges of her mouth and eyes were deeply etched with wrinkles.

The woman arched her brows. "Did no one *tell* you!"

Kaeldra shook her head.

"Hort's warts, why don't they tell the new ones these things! They send me a squip of know-nots and expect me to feed an army!" She thrust a metal scraping tool into Kaeldra's hand and gestured to some fat tube roots in the trough. "Well, what are you waiting for? Peel!" Kaeldra began to hack at a root as the woman scraped and muttered beside her. "They don't tell 'em anything, they don't feed 'em anything." She pinched Kaeldra's arm. "Why, you're skinny as a plucked chicken." She squinted hard at Kaeldra. "You look like a *girl.*"

Kaeldra gulped, her heart pounding. But the woman was scraping harder than before, in rhythm to her words. "And His *Lord*ship with his *stripe*-beast and his *horse*-with-long-neck—"

Kaeldra looked at her, puzzled.

The woman stared back. "You still don't know my meaning, do you?"

Again, Kaeldra shook her head.

The woman waved her scraper at the meat hunk,

which now was not much more than an enormous bare bone. "What do you think you were fixing to eat? A cow? A *pig*? Huh!" She snorted.

Kaeldra did not know. She could see now that the bone was much too massive to have come from any animal she knew.

"By the devil's rump, I wouldn't have stopped you, then. You're hungry enough, that's sure. No, my boy, that was a desert pig from deep in the land to the south. Though why they call a beast that size a pig, I'll never know. Never in my life have I seen a pig the size of a cottage, with ears like serving platters and a nose like a pit snake.

"He sends his men over sea and scarp and for what? Something new to stuff down that maw of his. Why he can't eat herring and squab like other fine folk, I'll never know. And now he's fit to be fried about this dragon girl and—"

Kaeldra's scraper slipped and dug into her finger.

"Watch yourself! Don't they teach you young ones anything?" She inspected Kaeldra's cut. "Tsch! It'll be all right. Suck the blood off, suck the blood off."

Kaeldra put her finger in her mouth. *Dragon girl.* She took it out. "What dragon girl?"

"What! You haven't heard! She's flittin' about the wood with seven half-grown dragons, or that's what they say. Some fiddlesham herb-and-leech man claims he saw 'em. Me, I don't credit a word of it. Dragons were killed off long before my time, thank the blessed stars. If these be dragons, they're the last of 'em. And His Lordship

150

says he *must* have dragon meat; he's rounded up a troop of men to go gallivantin' across the countryside searchin' for 'em. I say let 'em stay where they are! If there's a girl with seven dragons, she's a witch for certain and it'll come to no good stirrin' up the nest. And m'lady, with her blighted furs and feathers! *That* one won't rest till she has a gown of 'em."

"A gown of what?"

"Of dragon scales, what did you think! She wants—"

"Come here, boy!"

A man grabbed Kaeldra's sleeve.

"Well, it's to pourin' with you. Come back when you're done, and mayhap I can find you a bite o' dinner."

The man thrust at Kaeldra a huge pitcher, full to the brim with a dark, sweet-smelling brew. He pushed her through the back doorway into an even larger room, where a mob of men sat at long wooden tables, eating and drinking and setting up a din.

The heavy pitcher, seeming to acquire a life of its own, pitched and wobbled in her hands. Waves of brew sloshed over the sides, soaking her tunic.

"Pour!" someone yelled.

Kaeldra squeezed between the benches, pouring into upraised flagons, spilling often onto the floor reeds, already brew drenched and strewn with rancid meat. Perhaps now she could slip away and get back to the draclings—but how?

Kaeldra scanned the room. At the far end, seated at a table elevated upon a dais, a red-faced man huffed to his feet. He shouted and jabbed at the air with a joint of meat. Rolls of flab shivered at his neck, undulated across his belly.

"Draconitas!" he shouted.

A woman stood up beside him, the most striking woman Kaeldra had ever seen. On her head she wore a crown of tall feathers, azure and emerald and gold. At the tip of each was an enormous eye; when she moved, the eyes rippled and winked. A lush, white-gold fur hung from her shoulders and draped loosely to the floor. Her waist was girt about with a green-and-red snakeskin; her gown was of the hides of dappled fawns. Its bodice shimmered with some shimmery, black-and-yellow stuff: wildly exotic, yet familiar, too, somehow. Kaeldra worked her way nearer to the dais. It looked like—she sucked in her breath.

Butterflies. Row upon row of black-and-yellow butterflies.

"Draconitas!" the lord shouted again. He pointed at something high up on the walls.

"Draconitas!" the men roared back.

Kaeldra looked up to see plaques bearing the stuffed heads of animals, strange animals she had never seen. There were heads with striped fur, heads with spots. There were feathered heads and scaled heads, heads with twisted antlers, heads with horns growing right up out of their snouts.

And just above where the lord stood, mounted high up on the wall, was a plaque with no head at all.

"Draconitas!" The shout reverberated through the room.

And a tall figure strode down the central aisle, his scarlet cape billowing out behind him.

Kaeldra knew him at once. She did not have to see the gyrfalcon twisting restlessly on his wrist. She did not have to see his face.

He stepped onto the dais and conferred with the lord. The fat man nodded, looked at the gyrfalcon, then reached out to clasp the other's hand. As the dragonslayer turned to face the hall, Kaeldra felt the pitcher slipping from her hands.

It shattered against the floor, soaking her boots with brew.

The hall fell silent. Kaeldra looked up.

Jeorg was staring at her. He looked directly into her eyes, and she knew that he knew her. Her heartbeat rang loud in her ears, but she could not look away. She waited for him to speak, to point her out.

His gaze drifted across the hall. He turned and said something to the lord. The din rose again around her.

Trembling, Kaeldra bent to pick up the pieces of the pitcher. He had seen her. Why had he not betrayed her? She stacked the shards neatly in her hand. Nearby there was laughter and shouting. Suddenly her arm wrenched; someone yanked her to her feet.

A hand pulled down her hood, held up her plaited hair. With a shock, Kaeldra realized who it was.

"She is here!" Hokarth shouted. "The dragon girl is here!"

chapter 18

Yet often as the falcon nears, the dragon stills its
thoughts, and thus confounds the bird.
                                        —*Dragonslayer's Guyde*

Grabbing Kaeldra's plait at the nape of her neck, Hokarth steered her between the benches toward the central aisle. Her cheeks burned as she stumbled past the uplifted faces, now strangely silent.

"The dragon girl," someone whispered; others shrank back and muttered as she passed.

Jeorg, gazing at her in a way she did not understand, said nothing.

When they reached the aisle, Hokarth murmured, "Truly, I hate to do this. If you'd tell me where they are—"

"No!"

154

Hokarth shoved her in front of the dais. "This is the one of whom I spoke, Your Lordship," he said. "Her beasts—there were a dozen, at least—attacked me, unprovoked. Had I not dispatched six with poisonous darts and frightened the rest away, at this very moment I would be dead, gone, charred to a cinder."

"That's a lie!" Kaeldra cried.

"Silence!" Hokarth jerked her plait. Pain arced through her neck. Kaeldra drew back one foot and booted him on the shin.

"Ouch!" Hokarth yelped. He let go her hair and clutched at his leg. "Did you see that? She *kicked* me!"

Kaeldra ran for the kitchen, far across the room.

"After her, you durfdolts!" the butterfly lady screamed.

Several men rose and blocked her way. Kaeldra snatched a knife off the nearest table and held it out before her. "Stay back," she said, remembering the way the men had looked at her when Hokarth shoved her through the hall, "or—or I'll call my dragons."

The men hesitated.

"Cowards!" cried the lady. "She's nothing but a *girl!*"

One man lunged. Kaeldra dove beneath a table. Her hands slipped on the rushes; one elbow banged against the flagstones. Still clutching the knife, she crawled the length of the table toward the archway to the kitchen. There was a din of shouting and benches scraping. Feet kicked at her. Hands grabbed for her. Red, upside-down faces yelled at her.

A hand caught her tunic near her shoulder. She twisted and sank her teeth into flesh; there was a yowl, and the hand went away. She scrambled across the open floor, sprawled headlong beneath the next table. At the far end of the long, rough planking overhead, she could see an opening in the wall.

Almost there.

A hand gripped her boot. She shook her foot, smashed the hand against the floor, but it did not let go. She began to slip her foot out of its boot, but then her head whipped back in the opposite direction.

Someone had hold of her hair.

"I got her!" boomed a voice near her head.

"I had her first!"

Kaeldra tried to twist away but could not. Her scalp stung. The sinews in her neck stretched until she thought they would pop. She groped for the hand that held her hair, but it was near the end of the plait; she could not reach it. She was stuck, her boot held on one side of the table, her hair at the other.

"She's mine!"

"We'll see about that!"

And the hubbub swelled around her. Helpless, she was pulled first one way and then the other as her captors quarreled and others took sides. She gave a last, agonizing wrench, but to no avail. And it came to her, then, what she must do.

She wriggled her foot until it slipped from the heel of her boot. She held it there, part in, part out.

Then she sawed through her hair with the knife.

Bit by bit, the strands began to sever. Bit by bit, the pain eased in her head and neck. I should have let Granmyr do this, she thought, tears springing into her eyes.

As the last strands gave way, Kaeldra let go of her hair and slipped her foot out of its boot.

A roar went up, but she was already scrambling for the end of the table. She careened into a soldier stationed by the doorway. He grabbed her hand and tried to wrest her knife away; she dropped it and plunged past him into the kitchen.

"Stop her!" someone yelled.

The kitchen thralls stood frozen, staring. Kaeldra raced past them toward the outer door; then skidded to a halt as a band of castle guards clattered through it.

"Seize her! She's the dragon girl!" came a voice behind her.

Kaeldra whirled around to see a mob of soldiers rushing in from the great hall. The guards, brandishing swords, advanced in a rank from the outer door.

She was trapped. Frantic, Kaeldra scanned the kitchen for another way out.

The slop pit!

She darted past a table to the hole in the floor she'd seen earlier. The opening, wide enough for her to fit through, might be too narrow for most armored men. It was dark down there, but Kaeldra could see that the pit was deep and seemed to extend beyond the edges of the opening. Perhaps there was another outlet. A foul, rich, rotting odor wafted up; Kaeldra backed away.

"Seize her!"

"Quick!"

Kaeldra jumped. She landed with a splat, waist-deep in the moist, fetid swill. The stench made her gag. She thrashed about to extract herself from the mire: bones, fish heads, root peelings, eggshells, cinders, rotten carcasses, and maggot-infested fruit—all buzzing with flies and bound into a stew by a rancid, oozing slime. She slogged away from the hole, tripped, toppled forward, slithered down the mountain of slops, and slammed into something hard.

Pyro!

Startled, the dracling reared up, snorted out a blue smoke-puff. Then, recognizing Kaeldra, he began to thrum and flick his tongue.

"Pyro! What are you—"

Embyr and Synge appeared from behind a hummock of carrion. They scampered to her and, slimy with slop rot, leaped onto her lap. Their bellies bulged; their breath stank.

"You . . . you durfdolts," Kaeldra whispered, feeling an irrational surge of relief. "Where did you come from?"

Garbage, she saw, mounded clear to the walls of the room in which she found herself. But at one end, deeply shadowed, a passage led out.

There was a shout from above. Kaeldra dumped the draclings off her lap and clambered to her feet. ⟨Get out of here! Now!⟩

Another shout, then a soft plopping noise as someone dropped into the pit. The draclings bolted, Kaeldra close behind. More plops, then curses and thrashings about. The draclings had disappeared into the hallway; Kaeldra, squishing after, hoped they had not been seen. Although their stomachs bulged—they must have discovered this feast last night—they still trod lightly upon the slops. Kaeldra sank to her knees with every step.

Soon the garbage thinned to a slippery scum. Skidding around a corner, Kaeldra collided with the draclings at the head of a downward-curving stairway.

Kaeldra fled down the stairway, the draclings close beside. At first she could discern the shapes of the steps in the thin gray light, but as the stairway veered and twisted, the light was cut off. There was nothing to guide her but clammy walls against her fingertips and the cold, gritty feel of stone steps beneath her one bare foot. She plunged blindly down into a suffocating darkness, which was heavy with the smell of mildew and chilled by a penetrating damp.

Then came the sounds she dreaded: a crescendo of voices, a rumble of footsteps. The slop pit was probably not the only way into this place.

Kaeldra's knees buckled suddenly from an unexpected impact on her feet. The stairway had ended. Tentatively, she stepped forward, feeling the wall. The ground slanted downward, and the wall opened up to her right. Kaeldra turned to go that way, but a dracling became entangled in her legs; she lost her balance and sat down hard on the stone floor. And the draclings were nudging her, prodding her to the left. ⟨This way,⟩ they were saying, ⟨this way.⟩

Behind, the storm and clatter of the men grew

louder. No time to argue. Kaeldra bore left, feeling her way along the walls. She became aware of a gentle pressure of draclings at her knees, guiding her now to the left, now to the right, through a tangle of sloping passageways. She soon lost track of the turns they had taken, but the draclings never hesitated; they seemed to know exactly where to go.

Now the men's voices came from all around. Kaeldra could not tell whether they had broken into groups or whether the echoing walls only made it sound as though they had.

This must be a labyrinth, she realized. Granmyr had spoken of labyrinths, honeycombs of twisting tunnels through which the lord of a castle might escape if he remembered the way, but where invaders invariably floundered.

Did the lord's men know their way?

Did the draclings?

The air seemed to thicken, seemed to press against her. Her throat filled with dread.

She heard a clattering of footsteps close, and yet closer; she saw, through a passage that veered to the left, a flickering yellow light in the blackness. She pressed herself against a wall, and the soldiers went clanking past, only an arm's span from her face, dark shapes needle-pricked with light. Only when their sounds had receded to a distant echo, and when the glow from their lights had faded, did Kaeldra dare to breathe.

And then they were running again. Men swarmed through the tunnels on all sides; the sound of them was constant. Often Kaeldra and the draclings had to press themselves against a wall or duck into a nearby tunnel to avoid being discovered. Yet after a time the footsteps grew fainter, and the men were seldom seen.

⟨Wait.⟩

It was Embyr. For the first time that day, Kaeldra felt the dracling's fear. Over her own panting breath, she strained to hear.

The soldiers in the distance. The whir of a bat. A *plink* of dripping water.

⟨What is it?⟩ Kaeldra asked, reaching out with her mind to touch Embyr.

The ground swooned beneath her; Kaeldra leaned against the wall to keep her balance. The gyrfalcon?

She reached again to touch the dracling's mind, but felt the consciousness seeping out like water through a sieve, draining down to a place she could not find. She groped for the draclings with her hands and felt them—all three of them—crouching by her legs. She groped with her mind and felt silence.

There. A sound. Not in her mind, but in the tunnel. The crunch of a man's footsteps.

He moved slowly, not running as the others had done. Kaeldra strained her eyes to find the pale flickering of torchlight, but there was no breach in the darkness. He carried no light. Kaeldra strained her ears to place him: ahead, and to the right. She could not tell whether he searched in a different passageway or farther down in her own. She stepped forward with her bootless foot so as to make no noise, and moved her hand along the wall.

161

Ah. An opening.

"Can you feel the dragons? Are they here?" The voice was very close. Jeorg's voice.

There was a rustle of feathers. Kaeldra felt the breath of it across her cheek.

The gyrfalcon.

Her heart was beating so hard, she felt sure he must hear. She had to throw him off-track. She wished she had not lost the knife. She felt for her coin purse and closed one hand around the bottom of it to keep the coins from jingling. Then, fingers trembling, she fumbled with the thong.

There. It was untied.

Slowly, she coaxed the purse open. She did not know how the connecting passage angled off from her own, but she had to take a chance. She hurled the purse, heard it ring and clatter some distance away.

"Kaeldra?"

He sounded lonely, uncertain. She fought back a sudden urge to speak. It would be so easy. She would say—

"Kaeldra?" Pause. "Is that you?"

He is the dragonslayer. He is my enemy.

She held her breath as Jeorg's footsteps came closer, then began to recede.

She waited, her heart beating in her throat, until she could hear him no longer. Then the draclings were nudging her again, hurrying her along. The ground slanted steeply downward to another flight of steps. There was a glimmer of light, a breath of fish and brine, a muted hiss and rumble.

The tunnel narrowed, curved, and was suddenly flooded with blue luminescence and the sound of roaring water. Stars hung in the darkness ahead.

The cave, the one where they had spent the night. The draclings *had* known the way.

Embyr and Pyro loped ahead. Kaeldra waited for Synge. Soon the little dracling appeared limping behind her.

They stood at the cave mouth, drenched by spray. Surf surged against the rocks not far below, much higher than the previous night. And a small dark shape was wheeling above the waves.

"Kiree! Kiree!"

The kestrel.

The draclings nudged at Kaeldra, pushed her toward the water.

"No!" she cried. "I can't swim! Did you hear me? I can't—"

She clutched at the air as she slid down the rocks into the water.

chapter 19

In ev'ry fix I finds a friend;
In ev'ry brawl, a keg.
And so it is, when trouble brews
I drinks it to the dregs.

—Kragish sailor's chantey

The waves swallowed Kaeldra in a shock of bitter cold. They rushed up her nose, sucked her head under. She cried out for help and choked on a flood of salty water.

And then she was rising. She broke through the foam and gulped for air, her legs astraddle something—Pyro! She grabbed for his neck and hung on tight; he hissed through the waves like a giant eel. Embyr was ahead, she saw, and to the left a flash of lighter green. Synge. The draclings dove and leaped and arced, great manes of spume billowing and shimmering in the moonlight.

The water was so cold it burned. Kaeldra sat up, clinging to the spiny, flexible ridge that ran down Pyro's neck. Through the stinging salt spray, she saw the castle go drifting by. Tiny lights swarmed around it like sprybugs. The bluff gradually flattened into a long beach rimmed by the town wall. Ahead she made out the black silhouette of a ship against the evening sky.

The draclings slowed, making hardly a ripple as they approached the ship. The hull, encrusted with barnacles, loomed above. It rocked and moaned in the sea swells near the stone wharf where it was moored. The draclings swam round the ship, past the small square portholes, beneath the creaking hawsers that stretched to the wharf. Kaeldra looked up and found what she sought. Atop the mast, which swayed across a moonlit cloud, the kestrel perched.

Wouldn't you know it, she thought. The ship, no doubt, was bound for Kragrom. The kestrel led them infallibly toward their destination, heedless of the trouble it caused. What was trouble to the kestrel, who could fly off and reappear when all was well?

Voices. Footsteps thudded across the deck. The draclings slipped into the shadow of the hull and settled down into the icy water until only their nostrils showed. Kaeldra pressed herself flat against Pyro. She stifled a gasp as the water scalded her back with cold.

". . . only a fish, but better to make sure. Can't be too careful, with that ruckus on Rog," a voice said. A lantern bobbed on the ship's deck above, dripped puddles of molten gold upon the water. Kaeldra, not daring to move, followed the light with her eyes.

The sea made gentle slappings and suckings against the ship's hull. Far away, a dog barked.

Footsteps again, fading. Kaeldra let out her breath.

The draclings swam silently for shore in the shadow of the wharf. The surf carried them in in a breathtaking rush. Kaeldra waded through the shallows, her body throbbing with cold. She huddled with the draclings in the sand near the wharf and waited to see what they would do next.

But they only flicked their tongues at her and thrummed. Slowly, Kaeldra grew aware that they expected something. They were waiting, waiting for *her* to act.

Kaeldra sighed. Hugging herself against the cold, she rose to a crouch and peered over the edge of the wharf. It looked empty, save for a single mule-drawn cart and an assortment of wooden casks grouped near the ship.

⟨You stay here,⟩ she said, wondering why she bothered, for they always did exactly as they pleased, no matter what she said.

She climbed onto the wharf and tiptoed across it, feeling dangerously exposed. If the man with the lantern should come looking right now . . .

But he did not. The mule's ears twitched forward as she approached. It swished its tail and snorted. Kaeldra stroked its muzzle, murmuring, and soon the animal calmed.

There was no way to get on the ship. At least, not now. The gap between the ship and the wharf stretched as long as a man is tall. And if she did manage to jump it, the men inside would surely hear.

Kaeldra looked for the kestrel. It had moved from the mast and now perched in the confusion of rigging overhead. A massive hook dangled from the tangle of rope and swung back and forth above the deck.

A cargo hook, Kaeldra thought.

Cargo.

In the morning, the ship would load cargo from the wharf. The casks—they were cargo.

They were large casks, waist high. Large enough for a person to sit inside. Large enough for a dracling.

Kaeldra knocked on one cask and felt the fullness of it. She wrapped her arms around it and tried to lift it, but the cask would not budge.

Heavy. Full of liquid. Brew or wine, most likely.

She tugged at the chime hoop to see if it would come loose; a splinter slid beneath her nail. "Ouch!"

"Well, now, Coldran," came a voice from behind her. "And so we meet again."

Kaeldra whirled around. A man was sitting up in the cart. Thick, black eyebrows, graying hair—Yanil.

"You're a more convincin' boy without your braid, but I can't say I fancy your haircut. Where be your friends?"

She knew she should say something, should think of something quick. But her mind was stuck like a cart in a bog.

"Often I've been wonderin' about you," Yanil went on, moving down toward the casks. "Quite the rousin' exit you made. I wondered—could you be a witch? That would explain your hold over those dragons." He scratched his chin. "But you didn't seem a witch to me. You seemed—"

Kaeldra inched by the casks, ready to run.

"I wouldn't do that." She heard the iron in his voice. "I'll give the cry if you do, and you're well-known hereabouts, from what I gather." She stopped, and when Yanil spoke again his voice was gentler. "Your dragons ate three rabbits from my barn and killed my son's dog. I think you'll be owin' me your story, at least."

A light slanted suddenly across the wharf stones. Kaeldra dropped to her stomach behind the casks.

"Who goes there?" a voice cried.

"'Tis I," Yanil called out, in a lilting, slurred voice. "And Girtle, of course."

The light moved, spilled through the cracks between casks. Kaeldra's heartbeat hammered in her ears.

"Girtle? Where's Girtle?"

"Why, right before your eyes, man. There. Over there." From where she lay, Kaeldra could see Yanil clearly. He staggered back to his cart and stabbed a finger at the mule. "Girtle and I, we go way back. We've had many a long chat, me and Girtle girl, haven't we now? And she never nags or talks back, unlike some females I could mention. Does ye, now, Girtle? Does ye?" He patted the mule's rump. "No, you don't, there now, that's a good girl."

"Well . . ." The light did not move. Cold seeped up from the stones, numbed Kaeldra's chest and legs. Her tunic clung icily to her back. She bit down to silence the chattering of her teeth.

More footsteps. "What is it?" said another voice from the ship.

The first man muttered a response. "Old coot,"

Kaeldra heard, and "crack-brained," and "sampling his own wares."

The light shifted away, and Kaeldra heard their footsteps fade across the deck.

"You're shiverin'," Yanil whispered. "It's warmer in the cart. I'll lend you some blankets if you'll tell me how you came to be chaperoned by dragons."

She wanted to trust him, this kind-seeming man. She wanted him to think well of her, or at least not despise her. Perhaps if he knew everything . . . Anyway, she had little choice. She must trust him or he would betray her to the sentries.

The moon hung low in the sky when Kaeldra finished telling her story. Yanil scratched his chin and looked at her thoughtfully. "That was a stout thing you did," he said. "Gettin' the medicine for your sister. But I can't say I hold with what you're doin' now. Those beastlings—they may have been precious, but now they're gettin' big. They're gettin' perilous, as you saw yourself."

"But I'm taking them away," Kaeldra said. "I'm taking them away from people, to their kyn, where they will be safe. And," she added hastily, "to where people will be safe from them."

"Well, and I'm not so sure there be such a place. Not anymore. There was room for the Ancient Ones once, and splendid beasts they were. But now the world is full o' folk. No matter where you travel, seems like someone's got there first. The Ancient Ones, they can't abide near folk, you know that, missy. It's them killin'

169

our stock, and us killin' them, and them, bein' wild things, killin' back.

"I've heard tales of a dragon migration, but gave them no credit. I guessed the Ancient Ones were done in long ago. But supposin' there were such a place, where dragonkyn still live. How would you go about findin' it?"

"Landerath will know. The man I told you about."

"Aye, the man you've never met in the place you've never been."

Kaeldra swallowed. The ship creaked; the waves hissed and rumbled against the shore.

"And—you don't mind me askin', missy—what about yourself? When the lord's men find their way out of that labyrinth, you're in a royal vat o' brine. And another thing, about Rog. I've heard rumors of late, of strange goings-on about that place. Treason, an uprising, some suchlike. Not a profitable place to be."

Kaeldra pulled the blankets tighter around her.

"And I suppose they're close by, are they, as we sit and speak."

Kaeldra hesitated, then nodded.

Yanil sighed. "You know they'll be a menace, no matter where you take 'em. They're wild animals, like the wolf cubs my Gar once brought home. Cute as kittens, they were. Like a fool, I let the lad talk me into keepin' 'em—just till they grew a mite bigger, he said. But the wildness grows within 'em, no matter what you do. We kept 'em penned and their little bellies full, but within a half-moon they were killin' chickens. And dragons be a hundredfold worse, growin', as they do, to a monstrous size. And what on earth can feed 'em? Tell me that, now."

"I—I don't know," Kaeldra said. "But there must be something. . . . Landerath, he'll know."

"Aye, the man you've never met in the place you've never been."

It did sound hopeless when put like that. Kaeldra felt a sinking inside her. What would Yanil do now? Had she been wrong to trust him?

Yanil shook his head. "That fellow was right. I must be crack-brained."

Kaeldra looked up.

"I didn't kill those wolf cubs, though by the heavens I should have. I took 'em up to the high country. I don't suppose they stayed there. If my neighbors knew what I did, they'd have a lynchin' party with me as guest of honor.

"I'm thinkin' I owe you, for that you saved my Gar. But if I get you on this ship to Kragrom, you must promise not to loose those beastlings until you know they'll do no man harm. Do you promise that?"

"Oh, yes," Kaeldra said. "Yes, I promise."

Yanil sighed again. "You're a liar," he said, "and I'm crack-brained."

Kaeldra watched as Yanil pried the lids off four casks with an iron bar. Not all of the casks were full, he explained. He had already delivered a dozen to the castle and had picked up the empty casks from his last trip. Often, the casks were returned with circular hatches cut in their lids. Yanil hated this practice, for it ruined the casks for storing brew. Now, however, the altered casks suited his purpose.

Kaeldra's heart leaped at the loud creaks the lids made, and she glanced nervously toward the ship. But the sentry, perhaps believing it was just the old coot sampling more of his wares, did not appear.

"Well, and what do you think?" Yanil asked, inviting her to look inside a cask. "'Tisn't the Red Hart Inn, but it's travelin' your way."

It certainly was not an inn of any sort. The casks had seemed large from the outside. But now, as Kaeldra contemplated sitting in one, they seemed tiny and dark, full of a rank, sour odor.

She forced a smile. "This will do very well," she said.

"Perhaps some hay to pillow that hard wood?" Yanil did not wait for an answer, but pulled handfuls of hay from his cart and stuffed them into the cask. "And for the beastlings," he said, stuffing hay into the other three casks. "Now, perhaps you had better be callin' 'em, before the sun comes up and the both of us get thrown in the brig."

Kaeldra called for the draclings. Three heads appeared over the edge of the wharf. The draclings traipsed across the stone, eyeing Yanil. It seemed to Kaeldra that they had grown without her noticing; now they were longer than she was tall. Synge still limped, Kaeldra saw.

Girtle stamped and switched her tail. Yanil backed away. "You'll be tellin' them not to—"

"They won't hurt you," Kaeldra promised.

172

⟨You must get in here,⟩ she said, pointing at a cask, not at all certain that the draclings would obey.

Embyr reared up, resting her front talons on the rim of one cask. She sniffed at it, then sidled inside and curled up in the hay. She raised her head and flicked her tongue at Kaeldra. Relieved, Kaeldra scratched the dracling's throat.

⟨Come on, Pyro. You, too, Synge.⟩ They disappeared into the casks.

"Perhaps *you* had better set the lids on," Yanil said, with a wary glance at the draclings. Kaeldra did, and only then did Yanil come near. He tamped down the lids loosely, explaining that the draclings could push their way out if need be.

They can *burn* their way out if need be, Kaeldra thought. She could only hope that they would choose to accept their confinement.

Now it was her turn. Kaeldra unwrapped Yanil's blanket and held it out to him. "No," he said. He placed it back on her shoulders. "You'll be needin' it far more than I."

"Thank you." Kaeldra ducked her head so that Yanil would not see the tears welling in her eyes. She climbed into the cask. There was no way to get comfortable. She hadn't enough space to sit cross-legged and so had to draw her legs up tight against her. Even so, her feet— one booted, one bare—were jammed against the cask, bent at a painful angle.

"I wish I had a boot to lend you," Yanil said. He grinned, but his thick, black eyebrows pulled together in concern. "Here." He handed her a waterskin and a bulging cloth bundle that smelled of cheese.

"No, they're yours," Kaeldra said. "You've already been too kind."

"Take them," Yanil said gruffly. "I'll be off before you're aboard. I'll tamp your lid loose so you can push out and stretch your legs when it's safe. But take care, for there be many who seek you and mean you no good." He reached into the cask and grasped her shoulder.

"Thank you," she said, blinking.

"Good luck to you now." His voice was hoarse. Then the lid squeaked into place. She was alone.

She heard Yanil's boots clump across the wharf, heard the groan of the cart as he got in. Then all was silent, save for the creak of ropes, the slap and growl of waves.

Kaeldra mind-touched the draclings and found them asleep. They liked small, dark places. Perhaps she need not worry. She tasted a chunk of cheese, herb cheese, the kind Ryfenn made at home. And all at once she was flooded with it. Home. The hum of Granmyr's wheel. The milky smell of Lyf. Lambs prancing, stiff-legged, across a windswept graze.

The tears fell, then, salty, as if this *farin* sea were now a part of her.

Well, she didn't care. She would return to Elythia whether she belonged there or not. She would cross this blighted sea to Kragrom, and thence to Rog. She would find this Landerath, leave the draclings in his care.

And then she would go home.

Kaeldra felt for the draclings again. Still sleeping. They were safe inside the casks for now; and she was safe, too, in the dark, unseen. She rested her forehead on her knees. Just for a moment, she let her eyes close.

An ear-splitting racket awoke her: shouting, rumbling, screeching, banging. All at once she was tumbled onto her side and rolled over and over. Her cask stopped with a *crack*. Something heavy slammed into it, another cask, Kaeldra thought. There was a shout nearby and a harsh creaking noise, and she felt herself rising, swinging in the air.

Kaeldra, remembering the big hook she had seen, tried to piece together what was happening. The hook could not attach to the cask, so there must be a net of some sort. She felt things thudding against her cask: other casks, no doubt. The creakings probably came from a winch. The sailors must have rolled her cask into a net and were winching it up onto the ship.

The cask swayed sickeningly, then lurched to one side. Kaeldra waited for the sense of being lowered gradually to the deck. Instead, she heard another shout and a whirring sound. Her stomach lunged upward while the rest of her dropped. She smacked down hard, banging her head against the lid. Sunlight blinded her. She groped for the lid but her eyes could not see and her legs felt numb. Her hand touched something—not a lid, too small, not flat enough. A boot.

"Well, well," came a voice. "And what have we here?"

175

chapter 20

Whosoever shall Detain, Transport, and
Relinquish Alive one Green-eyed Dragon girl,
shall he Merit two-score Gold Croxains.

—Proclamation,
Lord Squamish of Regalch

Someone grabbed the back of Kaeldra's tunic and hauled her to her feet. But her legs felt as if they were made of wood. When the hands let go, her legs tottered and collapsed; she sprawled facedown on the deck.

"Get up, you, or I'll throw you overboard!"

Kaeldra saw the boot coming. She rolled away from it and, blinking against the light, struggled to her feet. Pain tingled in her toes and legs as the feeling flowed back.

"Stowing away, were you?" A stocky man with a full red beard gave her a shove. She stumbled and grabbed for a railing at the side of the ship. "No one stows on my ship. Now, git!"

The man pushed her along the railing toward a narrow plank, which slanted down to the wharf. Seamen tramped back and forth across it, lugging cargo into the ship. By now the pain in Kaeldra's legs had nearly subsided. When there was a gap between the sailors, she stepped up onto the plank—and then remembered.

The draclings. They were still in their casks.

"Please, milord—" she began, but a scream cut her off. Something swooped past Kaeldra and circled the ship, screeching.

The kestrel. A seaman aimed a crossbow, and before Kaeldra could call out, the bolt was arcing up through the sky. Bird and bolt converged slowly, like dancers in the harvest circle, then met at last with a muted *thunk*. There was an explosion of feathers; a small, dark object plummeted into the sea.

Kaeldra dodged the man and fled to the far side of the ship. There, in the water, floated the kestrel. It lay on its back, wings askew, the bolt protruding from its breast. Kaeldra stared down at it, unbelieving, her hands gripping the wooden railing. Then someone jerked her away, and the red-bearded man was squinting at her. "Haven't I seen you before?" he asked. He called over his shoulder, "Hey, Firth! Isn't this—"

A skinny, gap-toothed sailor sprinted toward them. Suddenly he stopped, moved his hand in the sign-against-evil, and backed away. "Captain," he whispered, "that there's the girl we seen in Squamish's hall. The dragon girl."

The captain whistled. "Squamish would part with a handful of gold for her, I'll wager."

177

"Heard you not? 'E offers two-score croxains for her. 'E's got a troop o' men waitin' for her to come out o' the labyrinth, on the bluff just north o' here."

"And more scouring the countryside, just in case. On the other hand—" The captain eyed Kaeldra speculatively.

"Which 'and is that, Captain?"

"I'll tell you, Firth. I hear King Urk's got men looking for a green-eyed lass like this one. A dragon-sayer, I hear. Now how many green-eyed lassies could there be?" The captain did not wait for an answer. "I'd wager my ballast those wenches are one and the same. I'd wager my keel that Urk'll pay a good bit more for her than Squamish will. What with the nasty business on Rog, this wench could be worth her weight in croxains."

King Urk! Kaeldra shuddered. Tales of King Urk's cruelty were fed to Elythian babies along with their mothers' milk.

But Firth was shaking his head. "You ask me, she'd be worth her weight in trouble. We'd have to take her all the way to Kragrom. And the monsters—where are they? I hear tell them dragon-sayers can *call* 'em."

"Don't be such a squeak mouse. We'll chain her below."

The captain yanked Kaeldra toward a hatch hole in the deck. She gave him a swift kick in the shin with her booted foot and tried to break away, but the captain only laughed. "That trick may work on that fat quack Hokarth," he said, "but it won't work on me."

He half carried, half dragged her down a ladder into

the dark, chilly hold, then dropped her onto a pile of sodden rope. "This should hold you," he said, clamping a manacle around her bare ankle. He slid a padlock through the hasp, snapped the lock shut and disappeared up the ladder.

Kaeldra tugged at the heavy iron chain that fastened the manacle to the mast. It held fast.

She was a prisoner.

The hold reeked of fish and brine and sour brew, but a draft of fresh air stirred her hair. Kaeldra looked up. Light trickled in through a square porthole above her head.

It was too small for her to fit through, even if she were not chained. But perhaps the draclings—

Where *were* the draclings? Kaeldra sought them with her thoughts. To her relief, she felt them nearby, somewhere in the hold. Thank the heavens *their* lids had held. ⟨Stay,⟩ she warned. ⟨Stay where you are.⟩

If only she had gone home when she'd had the chance. She was of no use to the draclings now that she was a prisoner and the kestrel . . . Kaeldra slumped down into the welter of rope, an aching in her chest.

Warily, she eyed the seamen who came and went through the hatch, bringing down casks and crates, baskets and bales. In the shadowed gloom of the hold, they looked like specters from the place-after-life of which Ryfenn often spoke, toting their burdens of sin. They regarded her with mild curiosity; Kaeldra guessed they had not been told who she was. Once, Firth approached timorously, as though *she* could breathe fire. He flung down a water jug and a pail containing a hunk of bread, then fled up the ladder.

Kaeldra gnawed at the stone-hard bread. A chill seeped up from the damp ropes and soaked through her clothes. She longed for the blanket Yanil had given her. Her one remaining boot chafed her heel and calf; perhaps it had shrunk. She pulled it off. The ship swayed in the swelling of the sea, and Kaeldra felt the first qualms of sickness.

After a time, the loading sounds stopped. The hold was packed with cargo, except for narrow pathways that wound between the stacks of crates and casks, and the small open area near the mast where Kaeldra sat. Someone bolted the hatch. Kaeldra heard a rattle, felt a thud, and surmised that the anchor had been weighed. Before long, the floor began to pitch and tilt. The cargo strained against the lines that secured it; one cask escaped and rumbled back and forth across the forward hold. A rat skittered out from behind a bale of wool. A spider shivered across her hand.

Kaeldra clutched at the rope on which she sat. The movement of the ship made her dizzy. Her breath tasted sour; her stomach heaved. She crawled to the bucket and was sick. Then she dragged herself back to the rope pile and collapsed in a miserable heap.

There was a tingling in her mind. Kaeldra looked up. She thought she saw a narrow head poke up from a cask. There, was that another? Yes, three of them, three slender shadows stepping lightly through the hold. The draclings sidled up to her, thrumming.

⟨I told you to stay. Stay! What if someone comes?⟩ They flicked their tongues at her, then curled up beside her on the rope.

Kaeldra sighed. ⟨I should know better by now.⟩

Kaeldra was roused from a fitful slumber by voices. The draclings! They must not be seen! She jumped to her feet and instantly regretted it. Her head felt as if something had broken loose and was rolling around inside. Her stomach churned. The ship heaved suddenly, pitching her to the floor.

"You can't do this!" someone was shouting. "I'm from the Sentinels at Rog!"

Kaeldra's heart lurched. She knew that voice. She raised her head in time to see the draclings slip through the dark hold and disappear behind a heap of crates.

"I don't give bilge water for your Sentinels." The captain's voice. "A thief is a thief. You're lucky I'm a gentle-hearted soul or I'd string you up."

"Wait till my master hears about this! He has friends at Urk's court. You'll be sorry!"

Kaeldra strained to see if it truly was the one she thought. She recognized the captain, who was climbing down the ladder, shoving another before him. She recognized Firth, who scrambled after. But she could not see the third person's face; could not tell for certain who it was.

"Hah! He's no good to you now." The captain again. "He was caught conspiring against the king. Urk's men stormed the Rogish fortress, and—"

"That's a lie!"

It *was* he. The dragonslayer. *How came he here?* She could see him now in the light that poured in through the hatch. He was coming toward her, but something was different. Something was wrong. He was staggering, and the captain and Firth held his arms.

"*You* may be a traitor, too, for all I know," the captain said. "What were you doing with those keys?"

Jeorg said nothing.

"Answer me, boy!" the captain bellowed.

Jeorg glared at him, defiant.

The captain planted a foot in Jeorg's back and shoved. Jeorg sprawled out on the floor beside Kaeldra; she scooted away.

"You'll tell me," the captain said, manacling Jeorg's foot to a second chain, "or you'll stay here till you rot. And I wouldn't try anything with the girl if I were you. *I* won't stop you, but she's got friends who'd make burning at the stake look pleasant." With a hearty laugh, the captain climbed up the ladder behind Firth.

Jeorg struggled to his hands and knees. "Kaeldra—" He did not seem surprised to see her. In the thin light that trickled through the porthole, Kaeldra could see that his face had been hurt. One eye was red and swollen; a nasty gash marked his cheek. She swallowed, strangely held by his gaze; she could neither speak nor look away.

The floor plunged. They both tumbled across the deck, chains ringing. Kaeldra crawled back to the rope pile and tried to sit up, but a sudden sharp roll of the ship knocked her onto her back. The hull pitched and swayed. An unlit lantern swung wildly overhead. Kaeldra closed her eyes and heard the rumble and crash of loose cargo, felt a freezing lash of spray as the world fell away beneath her and the sickness sloshed inside her belly. She hunched herself into a ball, beyond caring about Jeorg or the draclings, beyond caring whether she lived or died.

Sometime later she thought she heard her name. She had no idea how long she had lain there, but the floor was rocking in a regular rhythm, not pitching anymore.

"Kaeldra?"

There, again. She opened her eyes and drew in a sharp breath. Jeorg's face was inches from her own. He seemed tense, fearful.

"Look," he whispered.

Deep within the hold, peering around a stack of baled wool, were three pairs of slotted green eyes. Kaeldra sat up. The draclings moved toward her, sidling between bales and casks, now shadowed, now gleaming in the light from a porthole. Jeorg rose to a defensive crouch.

"It's all right," Kaeldra said.

The draclings rubbed against her, thrumming. Embyr glared at Jeorg. ⟨Bad man.⟩

Kaeldra glanced sideways at Jeorg, though she knew he could not have heard. ⟨He can't hurt you now,⟩ she said.

Embyr hunkered down beside her. Kaeldra scratched her eye ridges; the dracling kept one eye warily open and moved her head for Kaeldra to rub her cheeks, her throat, between her eyes. Pyro sprawled on his back, whistling softly.

Synge edged toward Jeorg, sniffed at him. His hands clenched, but he did not back away. The little dracling flicked her tongue then curled up beside him, thrumming.

Something moved in Jeorg's throat. Tentatively, he unclenched his hands. He moved one finger down Synge's back.

Kaeldra felt the strength seeping out of her. She snuggled into the rope pile and slept.

chapter 21

All creatures bleed the same blood, be they man or
be they beast. Our fates are intermingled.
Wheresoever spills the blood of any of earth's
creatures, there spills the blood of man.

—Private journals,
Landerath

In time, Kaeldra's sickness abated. She had no idea of
how long she had lain in a stupor, hardly venturing to
lift her head. She remembered little of the preceding
hours except for a few blurred images, which she might
only have dreamed: Jeorg giving her a drink of water,
Jeorg mopping her brow, the draclings nestling beside
her.

Now Kaeldra sat up and looked about her. Jeorg lay
sleeping on a welter of burlap nearby; the draclings were
nowhere in sight. Footsteps and voices sounded above;
a rancid, musty odor mingled with the smell of the sea.
She stumbled to the water jug and wet her parched

185

mouth, careful not to drink too fast. There was a hunk of banlep bread on the floor. Kaeldra, picking it up, found that she was famished. She broke off a chunk and ate it slowly, letting each bite dissolve in her mouth.

When she called for the draclings, they came bounding toward her through the maze of crates and casks and baskets, through the tines of light that entered the portholes and pierced the dark hold. They greeted her, flicked their tongues, then turned and scampered back the way they had come.

Kaeldra followed, dragging her chain across the open space, then threading over, around, and between piles of cargo until the chain pulled taut near a stack of baled wool.

The draclings were far back in the hold, scratching at a cask. She sensed a gleeful anticipation, a tantalizing hope for something good to eat.

Had they eaten? she wondered. They must have, else they would have awakened her with their complaints before now. But what?

The thought of food brought on a gnawing in her own belly; she clanked back to the open space, tore off another hunk of bread, and stuffed it into her mouth.

Jeorg moaned and turned toward her, still asleep. The gash on his cheek had closed, but a purplish bruise spread beneath his right eye. On his cheeks and chin was a sparse, light brown stubble. A lock of hair curled damply over one eye; his mouth was slightly open.

He looked so vulnerable, like a little boy. It was hard to believe that he was the one Kaeldra had fled and feared for so long.

She crept closer, remembering her dream, if it had been a dream, when he had offered her water. She recalled the tone of his voice when he had spoken her name, and the disturbing jolt she had felt when he looked into her eyes.

Perhaps Granmyr had been wrong about him. He had treated Kaeldra with kindness and, though he had pursued her, had neither harmed her nor betrayed her. Perhaps, she thought, he was not a dragonslayer after all, but a member of Landerath's secret underground, sworn to the saving of dragons. It was not he who had slain Fiora, but hunters from Elythia. Perhaps he only pretended to be a dragonslayer and in reality was protecting her. But Kaeldra could not think why he would not have told her this. Neither did she understand how he came to be on this ship, nor what sort of trouble he was in.

She reached out, hesitated, then gently brushed the hair from his brow. Jeorg stirred. His eyes opened. In a voice gravelly with sleep, he uttered her name. Kaeldra swallowed, her face suddenly hot. Her hand strayed to her own hair, and she remembered all at once how she must look, shorn and dirty, dressed like a boy.

Crash!

Kaeldra spun round. The draclings milled about a toppled cask, slurping brinefish from the floor. Kaeldra tensed, listening for shouts or a sudden change in the footsteps overhead. But apparently the sailors had not heard the crash or, if they had, thought nothing of it.

"They learned that trick yesterday," Jeorg said, sitting up. "In a moment, the fat one will likely—ah, there he goes."

Pyro, gobbling fish, burrowed inside the cask until only his rear legs and tail stuck out the top. He propelled it along the floor, crashing into crates, flopping over and over as the cask rolled with the movement of the ship. At last he emerged, dripping with brine. His swollen belly dragged upon the floor, and the corners of his mouth curved up in a self-satisfied smirk.

The draclings waddled to Kaeldra, thrumming, and they greeted Jeorg as well. Synge clambered into his lap; even Embyr rubbed against him. Their colors, Kaeldra saw, seemed to be changing. They were no longer quite so mottled. Pyro's coppery hue had deepened to a vibrant crimson; Synge was bluish green. Embyr's scales had darkened to the deep, rich green of a fir-shadowed lake.

Synge still limped badly—worse than Kaeldra had remembered. Kaeldra lifted her off Jeorg's lap and examined her wound. The shoulder had knit, but the new scales were soft and gray. They formed a scarred ridge, which seemed to pain her.

"What happened to this one?" Jeorg asked, scratching Synge's eye ridges.

"Her name is Synge. She was bitten by a dog. And this"—Kaeldra fingered the nick on Synge's back ridge—"is an old wolf bite."

"Is she all right?"

"I hope so," Kaeldra said, worried about Synge, and strangely agitated by Jeorg's gaze. She concentrated hard on Synge's wound, feeling Jeorg's eyes upon her, wanting to meet them, yet afraid.

All afternoon, an unfamiliar awkwardness possessed

her. She found it impossible to look at Jeorg, and their attempts at conversation were clumsy. Gone were his bluster and braggadocio; now he seemed as shy as she. It wasn't until evening, when shadows veiled their faces and the draclings curled up beside them, that the awkwardness began to ebb. Jeorg asked how Kaeldra had come aboard, and she found herself telling more than she had intended: about her ride through the sea, and Yanil, and the kestrel.

"And you?" she asked at last.

Jeorg told how the gyrfalcon had led him through the labyrinth. "She could feel the draclings' thoughts," he said. "But the draclings could sense my bird seeking them. They masked their thoughts, I think, for soon she lost them." Jeorg had blundered to the cave mouth at last, had climbed from ledge to ledge across the cliff until he arrived at the harbor. Spying the kestrel atop the mast, he had surmised that Kaeldra was aboard and had booked passage just as the ship was about to depart.

When he found that Kaeldra was imprisoned, Jeorg stole the captain's keys, thinking to release her. But the captain discovered they were missing. "There was a search," he said. "I was found out. Like a fool, I fought them all and"—Jeorg's voice grew soft—"they slew my bird.

"I lost, as you can see." Ruefully, he fingered his cheek. "You know the rest."

No, I don't, Kaeldra thought. I don't know who you truly are. I don't know why you have followed me, nor why you sought to release me. But a secret hope stirred inside her. The draclings—even Embyr—had accepted him. They would know, would they not, if he meant them harm? And the way Jeorg looked at her, the way he was looking now . . .

"You have told how you pursued me," Kaeldra said, and paused. "But not why."

Jeorg turned away. When he spoke again, his voice was low, and he did not meet her eyes.

"Uh, well. That's a long story."

"There is time."

"Well . . ." He looked at Kaeldra again. "I shouldn't tell you. You wouldn't understand."

"Maybe I will."

Jeorg sighed. "My father wanted me to be a warrior. Like my elder brothers. Like himself. So he sent me to be trained by a great warrior, as he had done with my brothers. I didn't do too badly, either, until—" Jeorg broke off, then continued in a rush. "He wanted me to kill a puppy. To strangle it bare-handed, as a test of ruthlessness and loyalty.

"I just—couldn't. And so," Jeorg continued, "he returned me home, dishonored.

"My father, not knowing what else to do with me, sent me to the Sentinels. I thought I had found my true calling because dragons . . ." He looked down, away from Kaeldra. "Dragons are evil; I could be ruthless with them, I thought. So when Landerath sent me with a message for your granmyr, and I surmised about the dragons, I determined to slay them myself. They would be my first. They would bring me glory, and overcome my

190

shame. I destroyed his letter to her, and—"

She was moving away from him, back across the open space as far as she could go. It wasn't right, what he was saying. She had thought, she had *wanted* him to say something else, something very different.

"Kaeldra—oh, I knew I shouldn't have told you! Listen, I didn't know you then; I didn't know *them*. These draclings—they are not as I had imagined. Now I don't know anymore what's true. They said Landerath is a traitor, and indeed he *did* say things that seemed strange, seemed—to permit another meaning. He was master of the Sentinels, and yet I cannot remember that he ever taught of slaying. Others did, Modin and Rowac, but not Landerath. He spoke often of the connectedness of things, of a common blood. His words seemed strange to me, but I didn't ask, didn't question, didn't want to hear. . . .

"And now they say that he is dead."

"Landerath?" Kaeldra said. "Landerath is *dead*?"

"The captain said so."

Kaeldra crouched among the bales of wool, her hands clutched into fists. Landerath couldn't be dead. For then even if she did manage to escape, there was no one in the whole wide world who could help.

"He was good to me, and I betrayed him. Perhaps if I had returned—oh, Kaeldra . . ." Jeorg started forward.

"Don't," she said. "Don't come near me. Stay where you are."

She did not speak to him again that night.

chapter 22

The traitor is unmasked; I know him.
—Private journals, Landerath

Early the next morning, they came to land. It seemed to Kaeldra that she had just dozed off when she was awakened by winches creaking, men shouting and tramping, loads thudding on the deck overhead. Sailors were moving through the hold, as well, she realized with a start. She jerked upright to warn the draclings, but they were nowhere in sight.

⟨Embyr?⟩

She felt an answering tingle.

⟨Stay,⟩ she warned.

The ship shook with activity. At least, Kaeldra thought, it had ceased its wretched rolling. She crept out from behind the stacks of baled wool to the open space where Jeorg sat hunched on the floor beside the rope pile. He looked at her and seemed about to say something, but she turned away, refusing to meet his eyes. Crouching on the opposite side of the cleared-out area, she watched the men.

They were unloading cargo. Had they arrived in Kragrom? Would she be sold to King Urk now?

The sailors lugged crates and casks through the gloomy hold and up the ladder into the brightness beyond the hatch. Some made jeering remarks to Jeorg, which he ignored. No one spoke to Kaeldra, although once or twice she thought she caught the movement of a hand in the sign-against-evil.

Soon, men came for the cargo just behind Kaeldra; she moved away. The cleared-out area spread toward the edges of the ship, toward the draclings.

Kaeldra felt a growing anxiety. What if they unloaded the entire ship, leaving no place for the draclings to hide? They could crawl back into the casks in which they had come, but she could not reach them to put on the lids. She willed the men to stop, to get out of the hold, to set sail again. They didn't. Yet in a little while they began to bring in new cargo, and the cleared-out area began to shrink.

The tightness eased in her shoulders and neck. Safe for now. But for how long? She had to do something, and soon. Sometime, they would empty the ship, and the draclings would have no place to hide. There was nothing she could do for herself; she was chained fast and at the mercy of whatever might befall her. But perhaps she could do one last thing for the draclings.

In time the flow of men into the hold diminished to a trickle, then stopped altogether. The hatch door slammed shut. She heard voices overhead, but not many, and surmised that most of the men had gone ashore.

Kaeldra pushed a crate beneath a porthole and climbed up. The hole was square, a little larger than her head. Her shoulders would not fit through it, though, even if she weren't chained. But the draclings—she had seen them squirm out of some very snug places. Perhaps they were narrow enough.

Looking out, Kaeldra saw that the ship was moored to a stone-built wharf, beyond which stood a small walled town. To the north curved a narrow, cliff-lined beach, strewn with boulders and heaps of sea-bleached logs. The cliffs were shrouded in a dreary, bluish gray mist, through which bulked the shadowy profiles of needlecone trees.

Kaeldra scooted the crate to the porthole at the opposite side of the ship, away from the wharf. She felt Jeorg looking at her, but pretended not to notice. Instead, she called for the draclings. They romped to her, thrumming through the half-lit gloom. Then, perversely, they ran to Jeorg and greeted him, too.

⟨Here! Come here!⟩ she said crossly. But they did not. Kaeldra dragged Pyro away from Jeorg and lugged him to her crate.

Ungrateful monsters, she thought. I don't know why I bother with them.

She grappled with Pyro, lifting him up toward the

194

porthole to see if he would fit through. But he twisted, flailed, wriggled out of her grasp, then scrambled behind Jeorg.

"Allow me," Jeorg said, tucking Pyro under his arm. "You want me to pitch him overboard or what?"

"No!" Kaeldra glared at Jeorg, not wanting to accept his help, yet knowing she must. "I just want to see if he fits through," she said finally.

He did. Jeorg pushed and the dracling somehow twisted and squeezed and wriggled until the largest part of his stomach had passed through the hole.

"Quick! Haul him back in before someone sees!"

Slowly, with Jeorg's help, Pyro worked his way back inside.

"Thank you," Kaeldra said, her eyes averted.

Jeorg inclined his head in a small, mocking bow.

Kaeldra tried to explain her plan to Embyr because the others always seemed to obey her. But it was difficult to make the dracling understand. Embyr kept asking where Kaeldra would be. ⟨Just swim that way, up the coast,⟩ Kaeldra said. ⟨I will come later.⟩

Embyr had trouble, as well, with the idea of carrying out an order sometime in the future. ⟨Now?⟩ she kept asking.

⟨No,⟩ Kaeldra said. ⟨Not now.⟩

Later, when the draclings were napping, Kaeldra thought about her plan. The draclings might be able to survive on their own for a little while, at least. They could forage for food in the sea; they seemed to have ceased floating in their sleep.

If Landerath were dead, what more could she do—even if she did manage to escape? Granmyr, she remembered, had said something about a council bluff. Something about summoning the dragons with a name. But Kaeldra had no idea where the bluff might be, nor what the name.

Still, she wouldn't send them away unless she absolutely must. If she did, she doubted she would see them ever again. Kaeldra did not know what would become of her charges if they escaped into the sea. The world was full of peril for draclings. But at least they would have a chance.

Over and over Kaeldra reviewed her plan, looking for flaws, keeping her thoughts busy, pushing back the fear that pressed against her heart: *And what is to happen to me?*

That night, there was a commotion outside. Shouts. Feet tramping on deck. The distant rumble of hoofbeats. Before Kaeldra could rise, Jeorg sprang to his feet and dashed to the wharf-side porthole. Kaeldra sat listening.

A shouted greeting. The jingle of riding gear. Jeorg cried out a word Kaeldra did not know, and then there was a thundering of footsteps above. The hatch opened with a creak. The light of many lanterns pricked the darkness, and a mass of people descended into the hold.

Kaeldra retreated into the shadows. The captain climbed down first, followed by a man in a flowing red robe, then a contingent of armed men.

"Is this the girl?" the man in red asked, approaching

Kaeldra. He walked with a limp, she saw.

"Modin!" Jeorg, his chain clanking, strode forward to embrace the man.

⟨Now?⟩ It was Embyr, hidden far back in the hold. ⟨No. Not now.⟩

"You know this man?" the captain asked.

The man disengaged himself from Jeorg's embrace, his eyes on Kaeldra. His robe, Kaeldra saw, was of velvet, richly embroidered in gold. A shag of grizzled hair frizzed out around the man's face, which looked gaunt and skull white in the light from his lantern. His eyes were lost in pools of darkness.

"He is known to me," the man said.

"Modin," Jeorg said, "by the Blade it's good to see you! I have been beaten and detained against my will. They have insulted me and Landerath. Tell them to release me at once. And"—he turned briefly toward Kaeldra—"the girl, as well. She has done nothing."

The man in red turned to the captain. He spoke softly, but there was a cutting edge beneath. "It is well you captured him. This man is one of Landerath's companions in treachery, plotting to bend the wrath of dragons to their own demented ends."

Jeorg looked as if he had been slapped. "But, Modin! You know me! I am no traitor!"

"I know very well what you are."

"Then I demand that you have me released. I am a vassal of the king!"

"Batten your jaws!" the captain bellowed. He turned to the man in red and said in an altogether different

197

tone, "I am honored to be of service, Sir Modin. Is there aught—"

Jeorg lunged at Modin, clutched at his robe. "Why are you lying? Tell him to release me. I'm no traitor!"

"Detain him." The man in red did not raise his voice, but his order galvanized his men. Three of them rushed forward and pulled Jeorg away while two more bound his hands behind his back.

The captain spoke. "Begging your pardon, milord, but may we expect some small, ah, recompense for capturing this traitor?"

"Certainly. You are bound for the capital, I assume?"

"Yes, we are sailing to Zarig, but—"

"You will find the king most generous."

"But, begging your leave, I thought that—*you* would take him. If he is as dangerous as you say—"

"I will leave my guards. Now, the girl—"

"Modin!" Jeorg cried, struggling to free himself. "You'll be sorry! I—"

One of the guards dealt him a brutal blow to the stomach. Jeorg grunted, sagging.

Kaeldra shrank back, afraid, as the man in red approached. He brought the lantern to her face; she blinked and turned away. "Look at me, my dear," he said. Beyond the lantern's glare, his features blurred and faded into darkness. "Ah, yes," he said. "Yes. You will come with me." He turned to one of his men. "Bind her hands." And to the captain: "Unshackle her foot."

"But—" the captain said. "The reward?"

"Ah, the reward." Modin reached into the folds of

his gown and took out a leather bag. He tossed it to the captain. "I trust that will suffice?"

The captain opened the bag. His eyes grew large. "Yes, milord. The king is very generous."

Kaeldra felt the cold metal slip off her foot at the same time the ropes gripped her hands. She glanced at Jeorg. He looked bewildered. Like a child, she thought. Like a little boy. All at once she longed to reach out to him, to sweep the hair from his eyes.

Stop that! she told herself fiercely. *Remember, he set out to kill dragons.*

But he has changed, an inner voice answered. *He would not do so now.*

⟨Now?⟩ It was Embyr.

Kaeldra's heart wrenched. It was time. The men were turned toward Kaeldra now; no one would notice the quiet movement in the dark behind their backs. And although she had planned for this moment, until now she had not truly believed it would come to pass.

⟨Now,⟩ Kaeldra said. ⟨Go now.⟩

chapter 23

Into man's domain,
To this high terrain
Where the spume of the sea circles round,

Through the northern sky,
Dragonkyn shall fly
When a girl with green eyes calls us down.

—Dragon to Kara,
The Promise,
A Drama in Three Acts

ḥold up!"

The man called Modin reined in his steed and pulled back on the lead with which he guided Kaeldra's mount.

When her mare at last jogged to a stop, Kaeldra relaxed the grip of her hands and thighs. Her legs trembled from clinging to the horse. Her hands were cramped. Beneath the coarse rope binding them, her wrists burned.

"Hold out your hands," Modin said.

Kaeldra saw the flash of a silver dagger in the moonlight and her mind went numb; her hands would not move.

"Hold them out."

The dagger flashed again. Kaeldra winced but felt no pain as her bonds peeled away. Gingerly, she fingered her wrists. The skin felt raw.

When she had emerged from the ship, this man had lifted her astride the horse and led her galloping through the night across the bluffs beside the sea. Kaeldra did not know how long they had ridden. It was not yet dawn, but her back and legs and hands felt as though they had been bouncing on that horse for a quarter-moon.

"I apologize for that," Modin said now. He was looking, Kaeldra saw, at her wrists. "But had I not bound you, they might have suspected."

Then he kicked his horse, still holding Kaeldra's lead, and she was left to wonder what he meant as they raced across the bluffs.

They came at last to a promontory high above the sea. The bitten moon illuminated a sandy track winding down to the beach in a hollow between two hills. Halfway down the track, sheltered by the hills and stands of needlecone trees, Modin tethered the horses. He helped Kaeldra dismount, then untied some animal skins from the saddlebags, spread them on the ground, and motioned for Kaeldra to sit. Limping, he began to forage for kindling.

I could escape now, Kaeldra thought. I could take a horse, ride away, find the draclings. She wondered why the man had left her there unfettered. Was he so certain she could not escape? Was he watching her? And what had he meant before about the others suspecting? And what had he meant about Jeorg being in league with

Landerath, using dragons for his own demented ends?

Kaeldra tried to make herself get up, but her body, limp with hunger and fatigue, seemed to have melted to the ground.

Modin soon returned, and before long a fire leaped and crackled nearby. He did not speak. Opening the saddlebags, he took out bread, cheese, and a packet of dried yellow fruits unfamiliar to Kaeldra. He spread them on a silver platter and set it down between them. He rummaged through his saddlebags and produced two silver goblets and a jar of wine.

Kaeldra's mouth watered. Her fingers itched to snatch a hunk of cheese and pop it into her mouth. Yet she did not trust this man; she feared to take his food. Even now he neither spoke nor looked at her. Was she a prisoner? Or not? A bubble of anger pressed up from her chest into her throat. If she were a prisoner, she wanted to know.

Modin poured wine into the goblets, lifted one toward her.

"What are you going to do with me? Kaeldra demanded.

Modin checked his arm, one eyebrow raised.

"Do?"

"Yes, do! You paid a sack of gold for me. Are you taking me to the king?"

"Of course not," he said, seeming surprised. "You're free to go. Although I'd hoped you'd share a meal with me. And I'd like to hear news of your granmyr. Landerath spoke of her often."

Kaeldra sprang to her feet. "Who *are* you?"

"I am called Modin, as you surely heard. However, I fear I may have misrepresented myself to those knaves on the ship. If they knew I was in league with Landerath, I'd be in chains or worse." He smiled, a quick, twisting movement that seemed to mock his words. "You really ought to have some wine. I find it quite calming."

"How do you know Granmyr?"

Modin drained his wine and answered as he poured himself more. "In truth, we've never met. But Landerath spoke of her so often, I feel we're old friends. Are you quite certain you won't join me?"

Kaeldra eyed him suspiciously. Was *he* among Landerath's underground? Modin's story had turned so sharp a corner, Kaeldra knew not what to think.

"Why did you take me here? What do you know of Landerath?"

Modin sighed and set down the hunk of cheese he was about to put in his mouth. "I can see I'm to have no peace until I explain certain events, some of which, I warn you, are quite unpleasant. But I insist that you at least sit whilst I do so."

Kaeldra hesitated.

"Sit! Sit!"

She crouched near the fire, ready to flee.

"Now, drink!" Modin held out the second goblet. "It isn't poisoned, my dear. We're on the same side."

Cautiously, Kaeldra sampled the wine. It was spiced with something pungent and unfamiliar, but she found that she liked it well. As Modin spoke, she nibbled at the things on the tray—after all, she reasoned, *he* had eaten them. The cheese tasted sharp; the strange yellow fruits were crusty and sweet.

Modin told how he had been Landerath's second-in-command at the fastness of the Sentinels. Outwardly, they had advanced King Urk's oft-repeated vow to rid the earth of dragons. But unbeknownst to the king, they led a small, secret society that sought to preserve dragons from annihilation.

"But why does the king campaign against dragons? They have been away for so long."

Modin shrugged. "Politics, mostly. It plays well with the farmers. And we all feel a primordial terror contemplating the Ancient Ones, don't we? They are creatures of the Chaos, anathema to civilization. As long as they live, so too lives the threat of their return. Urk also fears the green-eyed descendants of Kara, like yourself, all of whom have been, ah, banished. He fears you possess a magical power over dragons that you might one day wield against him."

Banished. Kaeldra shivered, thinking of her birthmother.

Modin's voice wove through the rumble of the surf and the stirring of needlecone boughs as he told how, when the banded bird had arrived, Landerath had sent Jeorg, his aide, with a message for Granmyr. "Jeorg was not yet initiated into the society; indeed, he knew not of its existence. Or so we believed. Yet Landerath was fond of the boy and thought he showed promise. I wanted to go to protect the dragons, yet Landerath said he could not spare me. There was a traitor among the brethren, he said, and I must help ferret him out.

"We gravely miscalculated." Modin looked down; shadows crept up his face. "Jeorg, I fear, had found out about our society. He sent a message to Urk, telling all he knew. Then he left for Elythia to slay the dragon."

"You know this for certain? About the message to King Urk?"

Modin nodded. "We have our informers as well. But we discovered his treachery too late. Urk sent an army, and the castle was razed. Landerath, unfortunately, died.

"I was away at the time and so escaped. But when the king finds that I have freed you, he will surely hunt me down."

"But Jeorg . . . I can't believe he would betray Landerath. Surely you might be mistaken?"

Modin shook his head.

"Then Landerath—is truly dead?"

"It is certain."

"Then we are lost," Kaeldra whispered.

"The society will rise again someday," Modin said, "although few dragons remain for it to protect, I fear. It is a great tragedy the hatchlings are dead. They may have been the last; the other eggs may have been destroyed. You, my dear, might have saved them."

"What?"

"The hatchlings. There must have been hatchlings. But they are surely dead by now. They could not long survive without their dam, and I have it from unimpeachable sources that she was killed."

"But if they *were* alive? How might I have saved them?"

Modin shrugged. "What is the use? They cannot be."

"But if they were?" Kaeldra insisted.

"You could call down the kyn of dragons."

Kaeldra stared.

"Know you not of the promise the dragons made to Kara-of-the-Green-Eyes? I am surprised your granmyr did not tell you of it, for Kara was kin to you. If a green-eyed girl—Kara herself, or one of her descendants—if such a one calls, they will come to her aid."

"You mean, if I called—dragons would come?"

"It's not quite so simple as that. You would have to call from where Kara summoned them—on the council bluff on Rog. I know the place and could take you to it. But the lore says you must call a dragon by name, and I know not their names. Landerath did, yet he told no one. Although perhaps you might manage without a name. . . ."

Modin shrugged. "But the hatchlings are dead, and you must yearn for home." He stood and untied the horse Kaeldra had ridden. "Here, take Wopra. I owe you this much at least; I feel half-responsible for luring you from your home."

But Kaeldra barely heard him.

Call down dragons? That was what Granmyr had said. And the council bluff . . .

Kaeldra thought of Fiora, the terrifying size of her, the blistering heat of her, the excruciating pain of her voice.

A whole *kyn* of them?

She *did* yearn—terribly—for home. But she had come this far. She had done things she had never dreamed she was capable of. Kaeldra looked out over the sea. The draclings were out there now, somewhere, waiting for her. . . .

"A pity, though," Modin was saying. "About the hatchlings—"

Could she trust him?

Kaeldra searched Modin's face for signs of cruelty or guile. But the sun, rising low in the sky behind him, kindled the edges of his hair, leaving his face deeply shadowed. He had known about Landerath's underground, she told herself. He had known about the calling and the council bluff. Perhaps he was mistaken about Jeorg—she hoped so. Nevertheless, Modin *must* be who he claimed to be.

"They're alive," Kaeldra said.

"Beg pardon, my dear?"

"The draclings. I was caring for them. They were in the ship. I told them—before I left—to go out the portholes and swim up the coast."

The firelight flared, and Kaeldra thought, just for a moment, she saw a smile twitch across Modin's face. But then it was gone.

"Why, that's splendid, my dear," Modin said. "You wouldn't, perchance, know the name of their dam?"

"Yes, but she's dead."

"Indeed. But the dragons would know her name, wouldn't they? They might come to that name."

Kaeldra nodded slowly. "It's possible. I don't know.

207

Nor do I know exactly where the draclings are."

"Perhaps," Modin put a finger to his lips, "perhaps you might call them?"

They left the horses and wound on foot down the narrow track to the sea. At the edge of the beach, Modin stopped.

"You had better go on alone, I think."

Kaeldra walked across the hard wet sand to where the broken waves surged and hissed. The wind slashed at her face, ached in her ears. The sea stretched, like an immense slab of shale, to the edges of the world.

Where were the draclings? How could she find them, in a sea so vast?

She and Modin had ridden northeast along the coast, and that was the direction in which she had sent the draclings. They could not have traveled as rapidly as the horses. Perhaps, Kaeldra thought, they were south and west of here.

⟨Embyr! Pyro! Synge!⟩ Kaeldra sent their names across the waves. She strained to see some sign of them: a flash of color, a burst of spray. But there was only the cold, gray sea, and the spreading pink stain of dawn. She strained to feel them in her mind, but heard only a crashing of waves, a shudder of wind, the thin, plaintive cry of a gull.

⟨Embyr! Pyro! Synge!⟩ A bitter loneliness swept through Kaeldra. How could she have let them go? How could she have thought she might find them again?

Something prickled at a corner of her mind. There

was a flash in the sea to the west, near the coastline. There. Again. And now she saw three dots above the water, growing larger and still larger. ⟨We come,⟩ Kaeldra felt, and, ⟨Coming,⟩ and, very faintly, ⟨Wait for me.⟩

"Here I am!" Kaeldra called out. "Here! Over here!"

Now she could make out their shapes, two ahead, one flying far behind. They wobbled above the water, rising and dipping in erratic spurts. Kaeldra gasped as one plummeted into the sea, then rose unsteadily into the air again.

Embyr came first, and Pyro just after. They skimmed across the surf, belched out flame and tumbled into the sand. Kaeldra ran to them. She tripped and sprawled headlong; Embyr and Pyro bounded on top of her, thrumming and flicking their tongues. Soon Synge was there too, lying in the sand beside her, sides heaving.

"You came," Kaeldra said, tears burning her eyes. "You came."

chapter 24

Torgar cut it out and spitted it on a branch. And when it was wele coked, he did byte into it. And sith that time, when Torgar ate that dragon heart, neither sword nor bolt colde byte him.

—*The Bok of Dragon*

Embyr did not like Modin.

She called him a "bad man" and refused to come near. But Pyro took food from him, and Synge often rubbed against his legs.

"Don't mind Embyr," Kaeldra said. "She didn't care for Jeorg either, at first, but after a time . . ." She trailed off, thinking of Jeorg. Perhaps Embyr had been right not to like him. But Kaeldra could not wholly believe it.

Modin shrugged. "It is well that it is wary. There are many who would do it harm." He packed the last of the provisions into the saddlebags and began to hobble the horses. In the early morning light, Modin did not seem as old as when Kaeldra had first seen him. Though he limped, he moved quickly and with a muscular kind of grace. Remembering how he had lifted her onto the horse, Kaeldra supposed that Modin's strength more than compensated for his one crippled leg.

He finished with the horses and led Kaeldra and the draclings down a steep path to a cave where he had stowed a coracle. Across a stretch of sea the island of Rog floated in a grayish haze. Modin dragged the tiny boat across the sand and into the shallows, motioning Kaeldra to get in. When she hesitated, he told her not to fear, that the coracle would rise above the surf. "But it will not hold all three draclings," he said. "They must swim. The island is not far, six sentares, no more."

Kaeldra sat down inside the coracle. It seemed tiny and frail, no match for the surf, which rose up out of the sea and heaved itself, foaming, at her. But when Modin strode through the breakers, pushing the coracle, it sliced through the curling spume and bobbed to the surface like a pyfal duck. At last Modin clambered, dripping, inside. He handed Kaeldra a hollowed-out gourd with which to bail, then began to paddle with sure, strong strokes.

The waves came at them like moving hills. When they rode to the top of one, Kaeldra could see the island ahead and the draclings swimming behind. But in the valleys between the waves, there was only the sea all about, dark and shiny as flaked obsidian.

Before long, Synge lagged far behind. "What ails that one?" Modin asked, his voice tinged with impatience.

"She was bitten by a dog. Her shoulder has not healed."

Modin ceased rowing to give Synge a chance to catch up, but when they glimpsed her between waves, she seemed not to be moving at all. At last, with an exasperated sigh, Modin turned the coracle back toward the dracling. Kaeldra wondered, as he paddled, if he were as impatient with his own debility as he seemed to be with Synge's. At last they hauled Synge in; she lay across Kaeldra's knees, sides heaving, eyes glazed. The wound, Kaeldra saw, had reopened and oozed green. And how will you get up that hill, my Syngeling, she wondered, turning her eyes to the fortress that perched atop a steep, flat-topped bluff at the island's crest. The haze had burned off, but a plume of black smoke trailed into the sky.

"I see smoke," Kaeldra told Modin. "I thought you said the king's men were gone."

"They are gone," Modin said. "It's only a fire they left burning."

Kaeldra, gazing at the solid column of smoke, wondered how he could be so sure.

They came at last into the lee of the island. The wind dropped. The seas calmed. They rode in on a wave, jumped out, and dragged the coracle onto the beach.

Kaeldra lugged Synge out of the boat and laid her in the sand. The dracling sprawled on her belly. Her shoulder still oozed. Embyr and Pyro plunged through the surf and circled Synge, snuffling.

"This way," Modin said. He did not pause, but headed across the beach for a track which wound up the hill.

"Come on, Syngeling," Kaeldra said. "We must go."

Synge lunged to her feet; then her legs crumpled beneath her.

"Couldn't I call them from here?" Kaeldra asked Modin.

"Only from the council bluff. That was the promise."

Kaeldra propped Synge on her feet, ran ahead a few steps. "Synge," she called. "Come here." The little dracling looked up mournfully, collapsed, and tucked her head beneath her wing. "Come on!" Kaeldra said.

(Hurts.) Kaeldra felt a sympathetic twinge of pain in her own shoulder. She stooped, picked up Synge, draped her like a woolen scarf across her neck and shoulders. Synge was light enough, but awkward to carry. A wing chafed against Kaeldra's ear; the dracling's tail flopped down past Kaeldra's knees and often became entangled in her legs.

They followed the track, which wound uphill through dry sea grasses and scrubby firs speckled here and there with nesting seabirds. When Kaeldra began to tire, Modin carried Synge. At a bend in the track, he turned off onto a narrower, rockier footpath, which scaled the slopes beneath the fortress through a thicket of celan trees.

"This will save us a couple of sentares, at least," he explained. But the going now was much rougher than before, especially with Synge. The path was so steep in places that they often had to grab onto roots and boulders to keep from slipping. Modin's limp grew worse. Kaeldra offered to bear the dracling, but fared no better; her unshod feet were lacerated and raw. At last they were forced to stop at the base of a steep, rocky embankment. She could climb it, Kaeldra knew, but not if she carried Synge.

"We're nearly there," Modin said. "The council bluff is just atop this slope. Why don't you go ahead with the other two? I'll stay here with the sick one. When the dragons come, you can send them for it."

Kaeldra looked up the slope, then at Modin. Uneasiness stirred inside her. "Why did you take us this way when you knew we could not reach the bluff?"

"It's so long since I came this way, I forgot how steep it is. In any event, the other way is worse. A storm washed out part of the track, and it would have been impassable to anyone carrying a burden."

Kaeldra hesitated. What Modin said made sense, and yet . . . A hard band constricted around her heart at the thought of leaving Synge.

Still, what else could she do? They would never make it back down carrying Synge, and if what Modin said about the other track were true . . .

Kaeldra knelt by Synge and grazed her cheek along the dracling's neck. Her scales were cool and smooth. Her breath was smoky-warm. (I have to go now, Syngeling.) Against her cheek, Kaeldra felt an answering thrum. (Modin will stay with you until I return. He will care for you. We will be together again soon.)

Synge flicked her tongue. Kaeldra kissed the dracling's eye ridges.

"Tend her well," she said to Modin.

"I will," he said. "Now, go!"

Kaeldra turned to climb the slope.

Embyr and Pyro reached the crest before she did. They scrambled nimbly upward, showering Kaeldra with loose pebbles and dust before disappearing over the ledge above her. At last Kaeldra pulled herself up onto a wide, flat expanse of rock. The council bluff. At the far end stood the fastness, eerily reminiscent of the castle Kaeldra had seen spring from Granmyr's clay—yet blackened, crumbling, smoking. The island fell away on all sides, surrounded by a wrinkled ring of sea.

Kaeldra turned to wave at Modin, but he and Synge were nowhere to be seen. He's taken her someplace where she can rest, Kaeldra told herself. Someplace nearby, someplace sheltered, where she can lie down.

The wind jostled her in fitful gusts. She struck out across the flat rock toward the draclings, who romped in circles, sniffing here and there, playfully nipping at each other. They spun round and galloped toward Kaeldra, careened into her; she tripped and stumbled to the ground. They clambered into her lap, thrumming, trying to find room to curl up. Something caught in Kaeldra's throat; how could she bear to let them go? When she called the dragons, she might set in motion forces that would take them from her forever. She cast about for another way, a way they could remain together. Perhaps she could stay here with them, away from people, letting them fish in the sea.

She looked north across the water, trying to stretch out that thought, trying to imagine what that life would be.

Something glinted at the fortress. Kaeldra, blinking, caught a fleeting movement on the battlements.

It's nothing, she thought. No one is there.

But men would return someday. And they would surely find her. If not Urk's soldiers, then other dragon foes. If not here, then elsewhere. The world was full of men, as Yanil had said. It was a dangerous place, too dangerous for draclings.

Kaeldra stood facing north and looked across the sea. The sun, no longer overhead, arced toward the horizon.

It was time to let them go.

⟨Fiora,⟩ she tried. ⟨Fiora.⟩

It wasn't right. Her inner voice sounded small and flat. Like a cowbell when she needed a gong.

She closed her eyes and tried to reach across the water, tried to imagine a kyn of dragons flying toward her. But, perversely, all she could picture was the draclings, the way they had wobbled over the water to her the night before, the way they had skimmed the surf and plummeted onto the sand. These dragons would be bigger, Kaeldra thought, their flight a burst of power. Kaeldra played with the image in her mind, stretching out the draclings, imagining the beat of their wings, the thunder of their fiery breaths, the curves of their necks and backs and tails; and she saw her, then, in the shape of her thoughts, she saw—

⟨Fiora. I call Fiora.⟩

There was a jolting in her mind, like an alien consciousness startled from its sleep. Warily she kept it in her ken, felt it sharpen into alertness.

216

All at once something burst inside her chest, exploded in brilliant shards of pain. The mind-presence fled; the draclings screamed and reeled as if stricken. They began to run: dizzily, clumsily away from her and toward the place where they had come up.

"Wait!" Kaeldra called. "Come back!" She reached to touch their minds; they were crying, the way they had when—

No. Kaeldra raced across the highland; the draclings plunged over the edge. She scrambled down the slope, sliding, an avalanche of pebbles mounting beneath her feet.

There was a quicksilver flash of draclings among the trees; Kaeldra set off in that direction. As she ran she slowly became aware of a chattering, a twittering, a keening, a cawing. There was something in the sky. . . .

Birds. The sky was thick with them. The air was shrill with them. It was like the other time, when Fiora—

No, Kaeldra thought. It isn't the same. It can't be. Synge is safe with Modin.

She pushed through a thicket, then saw them ahead. The draclings had stopped at last; they were sniffing at something on the ground. A man knelt beside them—not Modin—his hair and clothes were different.

Kaeldra slowed. The man looked up.

It was Jeorg. His face was streaked with tears.

"Kaeldra, I—" he began. He rose to his feet, and Kaeldra saw the limp, bloody shape stretched out upon the ground.

chapter 25

We are come to a time when, no longer cowed by the
old earth-powers, men must rise and take what we
need from the ancient race of monsters.

—Letter to Modin
Urk, King of Kragrom

K aeldra, wait."

Jeorg moved toward her, tried to stop her; but
Kaeldra pushed past him to kneel by the thing on the
ground.

It was Synge. Kaeldra drew her fingers along the
dracling's throat, seeking the life she knew must throb
there. She felt beneath a filmy wing, seeking the breath
she knew must rise there. Synge was still, too still.
Gently, Kaeldra turned her onto her back and saw the
bloody slit that cleaved the dracling's belly.

No.

Embyr and Pyro nudged at Synge as though trying

to wake her. Embyr turned to Kaeldra. ⟨Gone,⟩ she said, puzzled. ⟨All gone.⟩

"Kaeldra." Jeorg's voice was hoarse. "By all the gods I'm sorry."

"Sorry?" Kaeldra felt the rage pushing up inside her. "You did this! You always meant to do this!" She rushed at him, pounded his chest with her fists. "You're *not* sorry! Don't say you're sorry when you're not!"

Jeorg did not try to stop her; he encircled her with his arms. Kaeldra twisted away, sobbing.

"I didn't do it," Jeorg said. "I followed the birds and found her here, found Modin. He was—" Jeorg hesitated. "He had cut out her heart. He was eating it."

"You're *lying*."

"There is a legend that eating a dragon's heart makes a man invulnerable to the sword. Modin knew it and believed it."

"Then where is he?" Kaeldra demanded. It *couldn't* have been Modin. She had trusted him; she had left Synge in his care. "Why are you here and he is not?"

"When I came, he laughed at me, and ran away."

"Why would he run from you if he were invulnerable?"

Jeorg swiped at the hair in his eyes. "I—I don't know. Kaeldra, can't you see? I care for Synge. I care for you."

Kaeldra did not want to hear. She knelt and laid her head on Synge. The draclings sidled up to her, whining; she threw her arms around them.

She had failed. She had called the dragons, and

they had not come. She had left Synge, and now . . .

The draclings' sorrow pulsed against her own, a tremulous humming that reverberated in her bones. Something broke loose; there was a roaring in her ears.

Kaeldra looked up.

The horizon was moving. It tumbled toward them in a great long line, darkening the afternoon sky. The birds surged to meet it and the line broke into chunks, became a cloud of separate things.

"Dragons," she whispered. "They came."

They were every shade of green and red. They wheeled through the air in twisting spirals like enormous pennants set free from their moorings to swirl across the sky. They swooped above the island, circling, trailing wind spouts that thundered in the trees.

Above the bluff the circle of dragons tightened. A chaos of birds soared about them, squawking, twittering, screeching. The dragons hovered, waiting.

Waiting for *us*, Kaeldra thought.

She jumped to her feet. ⟨Let's go!⟩

Embyr and Pyro cowered behind her legs. She scooped them up, one under each arm, and staggered toward the embankment, fighting the wind, ducking flying branches and debris. She clambered up, ignoring the rocks that cut her feet and banged against her knees. The draclings squirmed fiercely; Pyro wriggled free. Kaeldra slipped on a patch of loose pebbles and Embyr bolted from her grasp.

⟨Come here!⟩ she called, but the draclings fled from her.

And the dragons spiraled higher, banked to the north. Were they leaving?

"Wait!" Kaeldra scrambled to the top of the slope. She ran toward the dragons, shouting, waving her arms.

One by one they saw her. They swiveled their heads to regard her, then twisted back toward the bluff in a long, curving stream.

The wind had abated. Kaeldra, heart thumping, knees weak, pounded across the highland toward the dragons.

There were twenty of them at least. They hovered in a circle that nearly spanned the bluff. Their scales glinted in the sun; their wings glowed with a pearly translucence; their bodies rippled in shifting currents of air. The largest dragon, long as a ship, so dark green as to be almost black, peeled off from the circle and sculled the air above Kaeldra. It glared down, its eyes vast, emerald pools, and she felt the power of its voice.

⟨Who called Fiora?⟩

It was a lightning bolt, a ball of fire, the beating of an enormous gong. Kaeldra fell to her knees, her hands covering her ears. Her head throbbed with the after-ring; she thought her skull would crack.

The dragon drifted nearer, spat out a whip of blue flame. Its breath-stench scorched her lungs. ⟨What is the death I feel?⟩

"Stop it!" Kaeldra cried. "You hurt me and I cannot think to speak."

The dragon lashed its tail; wind roared in Kaeldra's ears. ⟨If you would parley with dragons, you must pay

221

the price. What—⟩ The voice broke off. There was a humming sound, a strange vibration in her bones. Kaeldra looked up. The dragons had turned to regard something behind her. Their throats trembled; their wings fluttered rapidly. Kaeldra followed their gaze. Jeorg, one dracling tucked under each arm, stood at the edge of the highland. Gently, he set down the draclings.

⟨Come,⟩ Kaeldra called.

Embyr and Pyro looked up at the hovering dragons, then back at Kaeldra.

⟨Come.⟩

Slowly, Embyr tiptoed across the plain, muscles tense, eyes flitting back and forth between Kaeldra and the dragons. Pyro scuttled behind Jeorg and crouched in the shelter of his legs. Jeorg stepped away and nudged him with his boot; the dracling scampered to catch up with his sister.

The humming sound grew louder as the draclings approached Kaeldra. They flicked their tongues and wound around her legs, eyeing the dragons fearfully.

The green-black dragon dipped down, smooth as rippling water. Kaeldra held her breath as the massive slotted eyes surveyed the draclings. At last, the dragon rose a little, let out a steamy sigh. It turned to regard Kaeldra.

⟨Tell,⟩ it said, its voice harsh but no longer quite so painful. ⟨Tell about these.⟩

Kaeldra was not aware of telling a story in the usual way. She felt it flowing out of her in shifting patterns, like clouds that formed and combined and reformed and then were blown aside to make room for more. It began with Lyf's illness and moved through all that had happened since, until the pictures broke up and cleared from her mind, and she was aware, once more, of the dragon's gaze.

The dragon spoke. ⟨You have brought us the little ones; we are in your debt. For that, I offer my name: Byrn.⟩

Byrn turned toward Embyr and Pyro, who still twined around Kaeldra's legs. Kaeldra felt but did not understand the current of thought the dragon directed at them. Still, she sensed the tone of it, the tone of a she wolf's growl to her cubs, of a falcon's call to its chicks.

The draclings uncoiled from Kaeldra's legs. Tentatively they stretched their long necks upward toward Byrn, then all at once the air was rent by a high-pitched musical tone.

The draclings shuddered, then froze.

"What—?" Kaeldra spun round to find the source of the sound, of that shrill, continuous note. A file of soldiers marched out the fortress gate. They were led by a man on a horse. Some were armed with crossbows; others held something to their mouths. Pipes. Small silver pipes like the tone pipe Jeorg had. Kaeldra started to flee, but the stream of soldiers split; she stopped, confused. They marched no longer at her, but around her, forming an enormous encircling arc.

Far across the bluff, Jeorg let out a shout. He ran toward her, pointing up.

Kaeldra looked. Still hovering, the dragons seemed

sleepy. Their eyes were hooded, their wings slack. Slowly, as if dazed, they drifted toward the ground.

The man on the horse rode toward her. His mount pranced erratically, shying from the dragons; the man lashed it fiercely. It was Modin, she saw. Jeorg, still running, yelled at her; she could barely make out his words. Something about pipes. Something about a dance? No, a trance.

A *trance*. Kaeldra recalled the tale Jeorg had told about Porphy, the man who had momentarily tranced a dragon by means of a tone pipe. But these men had many pipes, and the tones would not be disrupted when one of them ran out of breath.

The bowmen were fitting bolts into their crossbows. They paused, bows aimed, as though waiting for orders.

"Embyr, wake up! Pyro! Listen to me!" Kaeldra shook the draclings, but their glazed expressions did not change; the cool, relentless pipe tone held them in its thrall.

"Byrn!" Kaeldra screamed. The big green dragon blinked when Kaeldra uttered her name, and she felt a stirring of hope. But then Byrn's eyes clouded again; she continued slowly to sink.

Modin reined in his horse beside Kaeldra. The stallion danced sideways, wild-eyed, nostrils flared. It snorted and tossed its head.

"What are they doing?" Kaeldra cried. "Tell them to stop!"

"My dear, I do regret this. It's nothing against your dragons, I assure you. It's just that we are losing the war against Vittongal and it would aid us greatly to have a corps of invincible men." He shrugged. "Unfortunately, this is the only way. Perhaps you should go elsewhere until it is done."

"No! Make them stop!"

"Stop? Now? After the days and nights I've spent plotting for this moment? After the years I've spent groveling before that sentimental fool Landerath?" Modin laughed, a short, hard bark. "No, my dear. I used you, but it might have been worse. Now if you'll just move out of the way—"

Kaeldra threw herself at Modin. His horse bucked and whinnied; Kaeldra stumbled and fell to the ground. Across the plateau she saw Jeorg wielding his sword against a group of soldiers. Then Modin yelled, "Loose!" and a hail of bolts swarmed upward, embedded themselves like tiny needles in the belly of a scarlet dragon. The dragon plunged to earth, grunting with pain, spurting blood; still it did not rouse from its trance.

A cheer went up from the bowmen. But the pipers did not join in; the piercing tone continued undiminished. There was a ratcheting sound as the men cocked their bows again. Kaeldra ran to the draclings, grabbed them, turned, careened into a soldier. He pried the draclings out of her grasp and flung them down. Clamping his arms around hers, he dragged her away. Then Jeorg's sword flashed against the man who held her; she was free.

"Loose!" Modin called.

Another rain of bolts; another dragon crashed down. Overhead, birds screamed and soared.

Kaeldra made for the draclings, but a soldier flung her down and sat on her. She lifted her head in time to see Jeorg rushing at Modin with his sword. "Fool!" Modin said. "I ate the lame one's heart. Your sword is powerless against me." Jeorg lunged at Modin. Modin laughed, and in that instant, when the older man let down his guard, Jeorg grabbed for the stallion's reins. He jerked hard. The horse screamed and reared, throwing Modin. Two soldiers seized Jeorg, knives at his throat.

"Wait," Modin said, struggling to his feet, his face flushed. "If he's so blessed fond of the beasts, let him watch." He turned to the bowmen.

"Loose!"

More bolts; another dragon fell.

They're slaughtering them, Kaeldra thought. They're going to kill them all. The draclings . . . She squirmed to free herself from the lout who sat on her back, but he was too heavy; she could not budge.

⟨Embyr! Pyro! Wake up!⟩ Kaeldra reached with her thoughts to find them and felt her mind sucked down through a silvery vortex of pipe sound. The world slipped away, a dim, echoing tumult of crashes and shouts and twitterings. She hurtled through a tunnel of bright, clear sound; she felt the draclings ahead—

"Kaeldra!"

She was wrenched away, and the draclings were gone. Kaeldra blinked. She was on the highland; Jeorg was calling her name. Modin stood by the draclings, glared down at her. Fear, for the first time, showed in his eyes.

"I can't allow you to do that," he said. He drew his

sword from its scabbard, pointed it at Embyr's neck.

She must bring them back.

⟨Embyr! Pyro!⟩ Kaeldra plunged into the mind-tunnel again, seeking the draclings, bending her thoughts toward them through the shrill pipe stream.

⟨Embyr! Pyro!⟩ Why could they not obey her, just this once? She called again and felt an answering nudge; then the pull of the current tugged them away. Again she called, swirling deeper and deeper until she reached them and touched them and would not let go. She broke through to a bright, soaring place where her body felt light and her breath tasted of smoke and her throat burned liquid-hot.

And a voice was calling . . .

"Kaeldra!"

It was calling . . .

And she was jerked backward through the stream, and the draclings came with her. The current surged and parted around them as if they were boulders in a rain-swollen rill. Then the draclings fell away; she felt the pressure of the soldier's knee against her back and the stab of a sharp rock beneath one arm. She heard Jeorg's voice:

"Kaeldra!"

And the draclings were rearing up at Modin.

Kaphoom!

A blaze of light engulfed him. He screamed horribly, consumed by flame. The pipe music thinned, broke, resumed in sporadic bursts, then ceased altogether as the soldiers gaped, aghast, at their leader.

A wounded dragon let out a piteous bellow; the

others began to rise. Through the flurry of birds Kaeldra saw the flash of dragon eyes, no longer glazed, but enraged.

Flame whooshed past her cheek. Kaeldra screamed; the soldier who held her fled. Flame rained in jagged ribbons from the sky. The soldiers were shouting now, running. There was a beating of air overhead. Kaeldra gathered the draclings to her, felt the rapid heartthrobs in their throats. They were all right. Modin had not harmed them. She must have found them more quickly than it had seemed.

The throng of soldiers dispersed around her. They were racing, Kaeldra saw, for the fortress, pursued in the air by flaming dragons. Three dragons lay dead upon the bluff. Blue smoke wafted up from the place where Modin had stood; it swirled away in the wind.

Then Jeorg stood beside her, apparently not badly hurt. Embyr and Pyro nuzzled him and flicked their tongues.

Slowly, Kaeldra stood. Her ears pounded; the ground felt unsteady beneath her feet. "I'm sorry for what I said before," Kaeldra said. "Your calling—it brought me back."

Jeorg nodded. "They say it is possible for a dragon-sayer to get lost. Do you know where you were?"

Kaeldra gazed at the dragons, who had driven the soldiers inside the ruined fortress and now circled, flaming, above it. "I felt what it is to be a dragon," she said.

Jeorg offered his hand; she grasped it and held tight.

A spray of bolts spewed up from the fortress and

clattered harmlessly upon the ground. With a burst of flame, the dragons turned in a twisting current and soared across the sky to hover above Kaeldra and Jeorg and Embyr and Pyro. Byrn dipped down and eyed the draclings. Again Kaeldra could not understand what she said, but a soothing tingle rippled through her mind.

Gingerly, Embyr stepped forward. She stopped, turned toward Kaeldra.

⟨Go,⟩ Kaeldra said.

The circle of hovering dragons tightened. A vibration rose around them like the hum of a thousand bees or the liquid sound of harp strings in the hills. Embyr looked up toward the dragons, then back again at Kaeldra. The dracling stepped away, puffed up, and floated into the air.

Pyro coiled around Kaeldra's legs. ⟨Go,⟩ Kaeldra said. Pyro whined and flicked his tongue. ⟨Go!⟩ Slowly, he uncoiled from her legs. He looked back in reproach. Kaeldra pointed sternly at the dragons. Pyro puffed up and bobbled upward.

The dragons glided down to welcome them, thrumming. Two green ones twirled in the air beneath the draclings, creating little swirling updrafts on which Embyr and Pyro bobbed like nutshells in a stream. A red dragon, Kaeldra saw, had gone down to find Synge and clasped the dracling's limp body in its talons. It laid Synge beside one of the fallen dragons. Then the others, mingling breath with blazing breath, set fire to their dead.

Kaeldra stood still, watched the luminous, blue flames lick the sky. Above the roaring pyre she heard the dragons keen: a singing ululation, steeped in sorrow. She blinked against the drifting smoke; tears streaked down her cheeks.

Then the dragonkyn began to spiral overhead. The wind picked up as they planed off in a great fluid sweep for the north.

Kaeldra felt Jeorg tug her hand. She watched the draclings shrink in the darkening sky. She strained to hear them, but could only feel the pulsing bone-throb of the dragonkyn in flight.

"Kaeldra, the soldiers. They may pursue us."

She let him pull her down the embankment and through the trees. When she looked over her shoulder, the bluff blocked the draclings from view. At last Kaeldra and Jeorg emerged on the road. Looking back, she could barely make out a dark, curving line on the horizon. And a familiar voice drifted, whisper faint, within her ken.

⟨Hungry,⟩ it said.

chapter 26

Carve out my name on the blackwood bole,
Carve out my croft from the stony loam,
Carve out my peace when the thunders roll:
Carve out a place for to call my home.
—Elythian folk song

Jeorg led her to a cove west of the place where she had come ashore with Modin. There, in a cleft between two boulders, Jeorg had stowed the shore boat he'd stolen from the merchant ship. "I had a friend among Modin's guards," he said, "and he helped me escape. He told me Modin had been seeking you and planned to take you here, to Rog."

It was nearly dark. They had seen no sign of pursuers; Jeorg thought it likely that with Modin dead the soldiers would lack a clear plan. Still, it was better to be safe. They must leave Rog, and soon.

Together they carried the boat over the rock-strewn

shore to the water. They pushed it through the surf and climbed inside.

Jeorg rowed. The sea was calm now, bereft of spume. Kaeldra watched the fire on the bluff as it faded to smoldering orange, watched the stars burn holes through the sky. There was an aching in her chest, as though she were hollowed out inside.

"They could not have stayed here," Jeorg said softly, seeming to know her thoughts. "Now they will be safe."

"All but Synge—" Kaeldra's throat closed up, and she could not finish.

"Kaeldra," Jeorg said. "I've been thinking. . . . Were it not for the birds that gathered around Synge, I would have gone directly to the fortress, would have been captured by Modin's men. I could not have warned you about the pipes. I could not have called you back." He paused. "Synge saved us all, by her death."

"It was a cruel exchange," Kaeldra whispered.

Jeorg nodded and said nothing.

"They shouldn't have had to leave!" she cried in sudden anger. "They have a right to be here! They belong to the earth as much as we!" Kaeldra hugged herself, shaken by sobs. The plash of water ceased; Jeorg enfolded her in his arms.

When her tears at last subsided, Jeorg asked, "And what will you do now, Kaeldra? Where will you go?"

"Home, to Elythia," she said. "And you?"

"I don't know," he said slowly. "I'm a disgrace to my family. I'm not sure I *want* to win their favor anymore. And now Landerath is dead—" He shook his head. "Oh,

Kaeldra, I was so stupid! He was trying to tell me all along, to tell me what you just said: that dragons belong here as much as we. He could not tell me directly, not until I was ready to hear. And I—an idiot!—did not comprehend his true meaning because I was determined to be a dragonslayer, a son my bloodthirsty father would deem worthy. And now it's too late. . . ."

Kaeldra's hand drew toward him, rested lightly upon his arm. "How is it you understand this now, when you did not before?"

"The draclings," he said. "When they came to me and nuzzled me and made that throbbing in their throats— Then when Synge—when I saw what Modin had done—" Jeorg swallowed and looked away. "Something Landerath said went through and through my mind. 'All things bleed the same blood,' he said, and at last I understood."

Jeorg fumbled inside his tunic and pulled something out: an enameled brooch, Kaeldra saw. It was pale blue, trimmed in gold, wrought in the shape of a dragonpod bloom.

"Landerath's brooch," she breathed. "Granmyr told me of this."

"He gave it to me as a talisman to show your granmyr." Jeorg began to unlace his boot. "I don't deserve to keep it." He tied the lace in a loop, stuck the brooch's pin through it and slipped it over Kaeldra's head.

"But this doesn't belong to me," Kaeldra said.

"Mirym told me you lost yours. You deserve it more than anyone."

Kaeldra held the brooch in her hand, ran her thumb across its smooth, enameled surface. Never had she seen an amulet so beautiful.

She looked up at Jeorg. "If you don't go home, where will you go?"

Jeorg shrugged, brushing his hair from his brow.

"Is there any place you *want* to go?"

"I—" Kaeldra saw in his eyes an entreaty he was too proud to voice. She remembered what he had said to her, before. *I care for you,* he had said. And she knew all at once that parting with him would leave an empty place inside her, just as parting with the draclings had done.

She pulled the thong back over her head and slipped it over his.

"But I mean for *you* to have it," he protested. "I'm giving it to you."

"And I," Kaeldra said, "am granting it to you."

They traveled on foot to Radnor, the town where the merchant ship had docked. Kaeldra stayed hidden in a burlnut grove while Jeorg made inquiries about a ship. He found a fisherman who—for a price—would take them across the Kragish Sea to a cove south of Regalch. They would buy horses, then, and take a southerly route overland so as not to cause a stir.

Without dragons, a dragon-sayer would be of little use to those who had pursued her in the past. Still, they deemed it best not to court trouble.

"Thanks be to Hort that my friend managed to return my gold," Jeorg said, untying a brightly colored bundle. "Our passage will be dear; and these were not cheap, either. Milady, your disguise." He unfurled a gown of deepest scarlet, embroidered in purple and green and gold. It was shorter than the gowns Kaeldra was accustomed to. He draped a multicolored sash across the gown and pointed to a pair of high leather boots.

"You'll look like a high-born Kragish damsel. No one who searches for you in those"—he nodded at the rags she now wore—"will recognize you."

"They're beautiful," Kaeldra said, fingering the fine, soft cloth. "But why did you pay so dearly for things I cannot wear in Elythia? They are too bright. People would stare."

"People *ought* to stare at you."

Kaeldra felt the blush creep up her face.

"I don't see why you always tried to make yourself look like something you weren't," Jeorg went on. "You aren't of Elythian descent. You're a Krag. Trying to make yourself into an Elythian is like trying to turn a dragon into a—a sun lizard. You, too, belong to the earth, you know."

Kaeldra thought of all the folk she had seen on this journey, folk of every height and girth and complexion.

I belong to the earth. She tried on the thought as she would try on a new gown. She had never considered it quite that way before.

One day in early fall they arrived at Granmyr's cottage. When they crested the last rise, Kaeldra caught her breath. A pale blue froth spilled down from the foothills and pooled like milk around the cottage.

"Dragonpod blooms!" Jeorg said. "A whole raving sea of dragonpod blooms!"

Kaeldra did not have time to marvel, for just then a shriek rent the air.

"Kaeldra! It's Kaeldra!"

And a thin, glossy-haired girl was running out to meet them. Kaeldra swung down off her horse and scooped up Lyf in her arms. She pulled away to look at her, at the shocking green of her eyes. Then Mirym was there, too, hugging and giggling in a most ungrown-up fashion. They took Kaeldra's hands and dragged her toward the cottage, where Granmyr and Ryfenn stood. Kaeldra gave Ryfenn a formal little hug, which was stiffly returned, then wrapped her arms around Granmyr, careful not to crush her. "Whatever have you done to your hair!" Granmyr said sternly, holding Kaeldra at arm's length. Then the old woman ducked and swiped at something in her eyes.

Kaeldra turned and took Jeorg's hand. "You remember Jeorg Sigrad," she began shyly.

But Granmyr was staring at his brooch. "You presume to wear this?" she asked. "Landerath's brooch?"

"Landerath is dead," Jeorg said gently. Granmyr flinched and shut her eyes. "I thought he would like Kaeldra to have it."

"And I granted it to him," Kaeldra finished.

"You can't do that." Ryfenn's mouth was tight. "It goes against tradition. You lost your own amulet;

you aren't permitted to grant another."

"I have done it," Kaeldra said. She held Ryfenn's gaze while the dragonpod blooms lapped against the hills; then, at last, Ryfenn looked away.

epilogue

The wild creatures of the earth are as milk for the human spirit; to destroy them is to starve our souls.
—Private journals, Landerath

$\mathcal{S}$hort of breath from running, Kaeldra burst into the clayhouse. She couldn't see her at first, for the sun had nearly set and darkness webbed the edges of the room.

"I should have thought," came Granmyr's voice, "that you'd be prompt. You've been hounding me to let you try this for so long."

Now Kaeldra made out Granmyr seated at a bench in the corner.

"I am sorry," she said. "Jeorg was banding birds. Some men from the eastern reaches came and had to take them right away. He says I'm the only one who can calm the birds, and he said it would take only a moment.

238

But then one bird escaped and we had to chase it all through the cottage. . . ." Kaeldra smiled, recalling how Jeorg had leaped through their cottage with a net, while the men from the east roared with laughter.

"That husband of yours seems to have found his occupation," Granmyr said.

True enough. Jeorg had not taken to farming, but he did have a way with animals. They gentled at the touch of his big, work-roughened hands; they obeyed at the sound of his voice. Men brought him their horses to be broken, their dogs to be trained for flock keeping. And now, two years after he and Kaeldra had returned from Rog, they had their own small string of horses.

Jeorg was famed as well for his skill with homing birds; but few guessed his true purpose in this. He had devoted himself in secret to continuing the work of Landerath: training the birds, banding them, sending them to outposts from which they would alert him of a dragon hatching. For he still had hopes of a hatching yet to come. He and a few trusted companions had vowed to watch over a lair if the time ever came, to protect the draclings by whatever means possible until they could fly north with their dam.

Now Kaeldra sat at the wheel. Her hands trembled as she slapped the wedged red clay onto the bat and moistened it with water. Long had she awaited this moment. She could not vision what she sought when Granmyr worked the clay, and so must work it herself. But now that Granmyr had at last deemed her ready, she was afraid. What if nothing happened?

Kaeldra's knees bumped against the rim; she had to splay her legs and hunch down over the clay. This wheel of Granmyr's had been too small for her since she began clay working over a year ago. But now, with the child growing inside her, it was more uncomfortable than ever.

"Left foot," Granmyr said.

Kaeldra kicked the spinner; her boot made a satisfying thud. She wore her boots high these days—Kragish style. She clothed herself in vibrant colors; she cropped her hair at her shoulders and let it coil as it pleased. Folk *had* stared at her at first, yet most seemed eventually to have grown accustomed to her unconventional garb. "I belong here," Kaeldra told herself whenever she felt the impulse to shrink and hide. "I will not be a sun lizard."

Now she leaned into the clay, feeling its cool, gritty wetness beneath her hands. It felt awkward, balky, moving in the wrong direction.

Center, Kaeldra thought. Center.

Gradually the clay grew compliant. She coaxed it to rise, then pushed down again until it no longer thumped against her hands but spun smoothly, without resistance.

"What now?" she asked.

"Make a bowl."

Kaeldra kicked again, then pressed two fingers into the center of the clay. It opened up like a blossom turned to the sun. Gently, she brought her hands together, feeling the wall rise and narrow between her fingers. It was a good bowl; she felt the centeredness of it in its wobble-free spin.

"Collapse it."

Kaeldra pushed against the wall, felt a resistance in the clay. She pushed harder. The clay closed in upon itself, lurched suddenly, seemed to tug against her fingers and rise of its own accord to form a mountain, a mountain chain. The landscape rolled beneath her hands, a strange, wild country, covered with ice. It tilted and pitched as though she soared through the air above it: cliffs and canyons, smooth snowy expanses of plain and floe and sea. Something dark in the distance: a cave? It *was* a cave; the earth opened up and she was hurtling down a high, dark passage into a cavern, an immense cavern, where a spring of turquoise water bubbled and steamed.

And there, in the warmth, in the sulphur-reeking, billowy-white mist, slept the draclings. Many dragons slept in that place—but Kaeldra saw Embyr and Pyro first, nestled in the curve of a big green dragon's tail. They had grown, Kaeldra saw. Never again would they squeeze through a porthole or curl up inside an empty cask.

As Kaeldra watched, Embyr lifted her head and looked about her, as though she had heard or felt something odd. She nudged Pyro; he, too, looked up. And a thrumming touched Kaeldra's mind, a ticklish vibration that grew stronger and still stronger until it hummed inside her bones.

Something shifted. The mists swirled past her, blurring the draclings. The cave began to shrink and slip away. No, not shrinking; Kaeldra was moving back: back through cavern, back through the passage, back across the chill, snow-driven expanse. She held on to the dwindling thrum for as long as she could, as though by clinging she could capture it forever in her mind.

And the earth slowed and grew stiff beneath her hands, and in the clayhouse it was dark. And the only hum was the sound of the wheel, slowing, slowing . . .

"Did you find what you sought?" Granmyr's voice.

Kaeldra nodded, unable, yet, to speak.

"Are they well?"

"Yes. But they are lost to us, Granmyr. They're in a strange place, unlike any I have heard of. And it is far, so far."

"Perhaps there will be others. This hatching cycle may not have run its course."

"But they'd only have to leave," Kaeldra said. "They can't stay here; we'd kill them."

"The Ancient Ones live," Granmyr said. "You've seen to that. A day may yet come when men appreciate what we have lost. Someday, if the Ancient Ones survive, they may return."

Someday.

Kaeldra's gaze drifted to the hills, where the dragonpod blooms, with their promise of fertility, rippled in the moonlight. They look so like milk, she thought. Like dragon's milk. Her hand strayed to her belly, and she felt a sudden joy: This child would wake to a world still touched by the splendor of dragons.

The Ancient Ones live. There may be others.

And that will have to do, Kaeldra thought, until *someday* comes to pass.

A remarkable fantasy sequence by Susan Cooper, described by *The Horn Book* as being "as rich and eloquent as a Beethoven symphony."

The Dark Is Rising
A Newbery Honor Book
0-689-71087-9 (rack)
0-689-82983-3 (digest)

The Grey King
Winner of the Newbery Medal
0-689-71089-5 (rack)
0-689-82984-1 (digest)

Greenwitch
0-689-71088-7

Silver on the Tree
0-689-71152-2

Over Sea, Under Stone
0-02-042785-9

The Dark Is Rising boxed set (includes all titles listed above)
0-02-042565-I

ALADDIN PAPERBACKS/SIMON & SCHUSTER CHILDREN'S PUBLISHING
www.SimonSaysKids.com

The magic continues with more fantasies from
Aladdin Paperbacks

**The Dragon
Chronicles
by Susan Fletcher**

Flight of the Dragon Kyn
0-689-81515-8

❏ *Dragon's Milk*
0-689-71623-0

❏ *Sign of the Dove*
0-689-82449-1

❏ *Mrs. Frisby and the
Rats of NIMH*
A Newbery Medal
Winner
❏ Robert C. O'Brien
0-689-71068-2

❏ *Silverwing*
Kenneth Oppel
0-689-82558-7

❏ *Bright Shadow*
Avi
0-689-71783-0

❏ *The Moorchild*
A Newbery Honor B
Eloise McGraw
0-689-82033-X

❏ *The Boggart*
Susan Cooper
0-689-80173-4

❏ *The Boggart and the
Monster*
Susan Cooper
0-689-82286-3

Aladdin Paperbacks
Simon & Schuster Children's Publishing
www.SimonSaysKids.com